CHRISTOPHER ARTINIAN

The End of Everything Book 1

Christopher Artinian

CHRISTOPHER ARTINIAN

Copyright © 2019 Christopher Artinian

ISBN: 9781090818645

CHRISTOPHER ARTINIAN

DEDICATION

To the family we have, and the family we have lost.

CHRISTOPHER ARTINIAN

ACKNOWLEDGEMENTS

To my wife, Tina. We are a partnership in every sense of the word, and if it wasn't for her, not one page could ever have been written. She works relentlessly to help me get my books to a wider audience, and I'd be lost without her.

Thank you to the members of the fan club across on Facebook. It is a privilege to be part of such a fantastic group, and not a day goes by where you guys don't put a smile on my face. Thank you, my friends.

And of course, the professionals. Sheila Shedd, my awesome editor who makes the impossible, possible with her metaphorical red pen. And not forgetting the amazing Christian Bentulan – He never ceases to amaze me with his work. Thank you, mate.

And last, but by no means least, I want to say a huge thank you to you for reading this book. I've said this before, but it is as true now as it ever was: Time is not something we get back, and for someone to spend theirs reading one of my books makes me feel immensely proud and very humble at the same time. It is a feeling I will never get used to, and never take for granted. Many, many thanks.

1

The banging against the thick pine door had stopped over thirty minutes ago, but Wren was still sat in one corner of the room with her knees tucked up to her chest, gently rocking back and forth. Her eyes were fixed firmly on the entrance, which she had wedged shut by turning her bed on its side and squeezing it into place, scuffing the skirting board and tearing big swathes of wallpaper. Her tears were nothing more than salty trails on both cheeks now, but it would not take much for the torrents to start again. The newly double-glazed windows could only block out so much of the terror from outside as screams echoed around the usually quiet suburb.

Less than an hour before, she had been downstairs with her family, preparing for their journey north, and now...now this. Wren climbed to her feet but kept her back to the wall. The wall gave her comfort. With the wall behind her, she did not need eyes in the back of her head.

"Brian! Please, no!" came the petrified scream from outside.

Brian was Wren's neighbour, next door but one. The voice that had shouted was quivery, broken, but most of all terrified, and it sounded like Brian's partner, Catriona. Wren edged to the window and peered out through the slit in the blinds. She could see Catriona, backing down the street, looking towards the door to her house. Because of the angle, Wren could not see what Catriona was looking at. Suddenly, the terrified woman turned and began to run, letting out another chilling scream.

Brian, or what used to be Brian, ran from the house and down their garden path, hurtling towards Catriona. With each stride he gained on her, and as he leapt through the air and his hands grabbed Catriona's shoulders, Wren pulled back from the window. A blood-curdling scream ricocheted up and down the street. Wren let out a whimper and slid back down to the floor, folding her arms tightly around herself. She began to rock back and forth once again.

In the distance, the sound of gunfire rang out. Sustained volleys continued for some time before diminishing and then going silent. Wren remained on the floor, hoping that she was going to wake up soon and it was all just a horrible nightmare.

She did not know how long she had been sat shaking before she realised she needed to pee. The bathroom was at the end of the landing, a mere few feet away from her bedroom door, but...but she didn't know if her family was still in the house. Her family had undergone the metamorphosis that millions, if not billions of others had. They were not her family anymore. Now they were something else. It started with a bite and in no time at all.... Her eyes filled with tears again.

She knew she would have to face these creatures at some point, but it was too soon. It was too soon to open that door. Wren grabbed the small plastic bin that sat underneath her desk, she took out the torn up envelopes and the empty biro, and placed the bin back down on the carpet. She carefully unbuttoned her jeans and crouched over the receptacle. She let out a long sigh and squatted there for several seconds before the sound of water spraying against plastic began.

When she had finished, she buttoned her jeans and carried the bucket across to the window. She looked up and down the street but saw no one. As quietly as she could, she levered the blinds to one side, pulled up the handle on the UPVC window and opened it. The faintest squeak sounded and she paused, fearful that something outside her door had heard her and a barrage of bangs and thuds would begin once again. When nothing happened, she pushed the window open a little further and tipped out the contents of the bucket. Her nose creased a little as the yellow liquid flowed out of the opaque plastic bin and splashed onto the paving slabs below. When the final drops had drained, she pulled the window shut and placed the bin back underneath her desk.

There was still a slight smell of urine in the room, but she would rather endure that than face whatever fate awaited her out on the landing. Wren heard the screech of tyres and rushed back to the window. A van sped down the street, smashing the wing mirror of a parked car as it went. Reflective glass flew into the air almost in slow motion. As it smashed into smaller pieces on the ground, the van's tyres screeched again, taking a bend way too fast, hitting the kerb and cartwheeling over a garden fence before destroying the front of a house in an explosion of glass and masonry.

Wren let out a frightened gasp to see such horror. What had caused the occupant of the van to drive so recklessly? Then she saw them. More than a dozen of the creatures sprinted down the street in the direction of the crashed vehicle. Like ants crawling greedily over a piece of discarded food, they stumbled around and over the van to get to any living prey. Despite the thick glass, Wren heard the bone-chilling scream of a woman, presumably being attacked by one of those *things*. Wren stepped back from the window. She had no idea what to do, or where to go.

She turned around and looked at her trophy shelves. All that work, and now it was for nothing. She was going to be in the squad for the next Commonwealth Games, but now…all that training…all those early mornings and late nights…she had missed out on parties and fun and boys…all for the chance to compete. Had it all been for nothing?

Wren paced up and down her room, trying to tread lightly and remembering to avoid the creaky floorboards. She could not stay in there forever; she would have to make a break for it sooner or later. Her mother and father had decided that the family were going to travel north, to Inverness. Wren's grandad lived up there. The theory was that the fewer people there were, the safer it would be, and Inverness had about a tenth the population of Edinburgh. It seemed like sound logic.

Wren paused in front of her shelf. She looked at the trophies and medals one last time, then turned to look at her bedroom door. "Screw this," she said, marching across the floor, creaky floorboards and all. She stood by the upturned bed for a few seconds before banging hard on the door, one, two, three times. Then she waited…and waited. There were no charging feet, no volley of battering fists and hands, there was nothing.

Wren stood there a full minute just listening, but did not hear anything that suggested there was someone in the house other than herself. She struck the door with her palm three more times and waited another minute. She was greeted only by silence.

She let out a deep sigh before beginning to drag the bed away from the door. It was wedged hard, and in the end, she had to leapfrog over and put her back against it to push it out of the way. She moved it back close to its usual position and went to stand back at the door. She took a tight hold of the handle, closed her eyes, and whispered a small prayer. As she opened them again, she levered the handle down and pulled the door inwards. The landing was clear. She stepped out of the room, leaving the door ajar.

Now, out of the confines and safety of her bedroom, she was not so brave. She tiptoed across the landing, peeking through each open door as she went. Upstairs was most definitely devoid of anyone but her. She walked into the bathroom and cupped her hand underneath the cold water tap, taking a couple of good drinks before heading back along the landing and to the staircase.

She looked down the thirteen carpeted stairs, and a torrent of memories came flooding back to her. This was the house she had grown up in, and now, she would always remember it as the house her family had died in. She began to move, taking a firm hold of the bannister as she went. One foot after another, she descended the stairs, then she came to a sudden stop as the seventh step let out a creak that sliced through the silence like a scythe. Wren stayed there frozen as the seconds dragged into a minute, but nothing came out of the shadows to meet her. She continued her journey down until she hit the solid surface of the hall floor. Wren looked right, to the small entrance hall and back door, then turned left. She popped her head around the corner of the small toilet; it was empty. She stepped into the large kitchen diner. The front door was still wide open. The family had been loading the car when it happened, when their world had come to a sudden end. She hoped they were all gone now. What she would not give to see them again, but as their old selves, not the new form they had taken. As Wren approached the door, she tiptoed to look over the breakfast bar; there was definitely nobody left behind.

She closed the front door and turned the key in the lock, placing her back firmly against it and letting out a sigh of relief. A scream pierced the distant air and Wren didn't feel quite so relieved any more. She headed back out of the kitchen and down the long hallway to the living room. She was about to open the door when a hollow *thud* from inside turned her blood to ice.

She ran back into the kitchen and opened a drawer, pulling out a long carving knife. There was nobody left to protect her. She had seen what had happened to her mother and father; she would never forget those images, ever. Now, whatever was waiting for her in the living room was something she would have to face by herself. More than face, though, she would have to deal with it. If it was one of those creatures, if it was a reanimated corpse, no matter whose face it wore, it was no longer human. She would have to learn that, otherwise risk turning into one herself.

She stepped back out into the hallway as something clattered on the floor in the living room. Wren held the handle of the knife in both hands, pointing it towards the door, as if trying to ward off whatever evil lay behind it. Another *thud* came from inside, and she could feel her heart beating faster and her legs begin to quake with fear as she placed her fingers on the door handle. She would have to act fast—she had seen how quickly those things moved. A memory flashed across her vision; she and her sister, Robyn, sneaking downstairs when she was just eleven to watch a late-night horror movie. It was a black and white zombie film from the sixties, and it was scary as hell. What Wren wouldn't give to face those clumsy, slow-moving, living dead things now, rather than these...monsters.

She held her breath. One...two...three, before bursting through the door. The afternoon sun almost blinded her as she stormed into the living room from the dark hallway. A figure stood in the bay window, silhouetted against the backdrop of the white lace curtains. *No time to think—charge.* Wren ran towards it, letting out a banshee-like howl, but the figure remained still until it put its hands up in front of itself defensively.

"Wren!" it shouted, dropping a large wrought iron candlestick holder on the floor.

Wren stopped in her tracks, letting her eyes focus. The adrenalin was still pumping and her heart was pounding, but she managed to reel in her primal instincts. "*Robyn?*" Wren looked at the knife in her hand before dropping it on the floor with a look of pure horror on her face. She had nearly killed her sister. "Oh, Robyn," she said, throwing her arms around her sibling and squeezing her tight. The pair of them began to sob. They had both seen what had happened to their mother and father, they had both fled, each assuming the other had fallen victim to the virus. Now, suddenly, they were able to savour the happiness of finding one another alive. They stayed like that for over a minute and when they pulled back, their eyes were red their faces streaked with salty tears.

"I heard noise in here; I thought it was one of those things," Wren said, finally finding her voice.

"I was looking for a weapon; the candlestick holder was all I could find. It has a spike on the end," her sister replied.

"Didn't you hear me earlier?"

"I thought you were one of them! I've been in this room ever since this morning."

"Did you see the van?"

"I heard it. Then I saw those things. Most of the time, I've been hiding behind the sofa. They were banging on your door forever…then it all stopped. That's when I thought they'd got you too."

"I wedged my bed against the entrance. They couldn't get in."

"I wedged the sofa against this one. I pulled it away about an hour ago and I've been trying to build up the courage to head out ever since. I was hungry, but I heard noise in the kitchen. I tried to stay as quiet as I could, hoping whatever it was would head out again. If I'd have tried to push the sofa back, I'd have been heard for sure."

"I locked the front door. We're safe for the time being."

Wren was fifteen, Robyn was seventeen; they looked very similar but for the fact Wren still had her natural blonde hair which she tied back in a ponytail, while Robyn had cropped hers a bit shorter and dyed it black. "You want a sandwich?" asked Wren as she headed into the kitchen.

"Yeah."

There was no electricity, but the water was still running for the time being. She made two potted meat sandwiches and put them on the kitchen table. She poured two glasses of juice and handed one to Robyn as she came in.

The two of them sat down and began to stuff the food into their mouths; they were starving. They finished the sandwiches in no time, then went to make two more. When they were finally finished eating and drinking, they headed upstairs to Robyn's room, where she got changed into fresh clothes. "We need to decide what we're going to do," Robyn said, as Wren sat on the bed.

"I think we should stick with the original plan. I think we should head to Grandad's. It makes sense—less people, less danger."

"And how do you propose we do that? Neither of us can drive and Inverness is over a hundred and fifty miles away."

"We can't stay here," Wren shrugged.

"I don't disagree. But Inverness?"

"Where then?"

Robyn went quiet. "I don't know."

"Look. It's not as mad as it sounds," Wren said. "We do it in stages. There are, like, over four hundred thousand people in Edinburgh. Inverness? Maybe forty? Fifty thousand? That alone makes it a lot safer."

"Oh yeah, you're absolutely right. Instead of fighting four hundred thousand zombies, we'd only have to fight forty thousand. It's a real no brainer," Robyn said, pulling on a fresh t-shirt.

"Well, you come up with an idea then. But think about it; Grandad can do anything. He can build anything. If anyone could get through this thing, it's him."

"Once again, I agree with you, but, and this is an important but, IT'S ONE HUNDRED AND FIFTY MILES AWAY!!!"

"Look, sis. You and me are very different, I get that. But I also know we can do this," Wren said, standing up and heading to the door. "I'm going to get my rucksack and start packing."

"I've not said I'm going."

"Look. There are some things we can agree on. Mum and Dad aren't coming back. You and I are still alive, but we won't be for long if we stay here. We need to get out of the city. Yes or no? Do you agree with all those points?" Wren asked.

Robyn sat down on the bed and thought for a moment as she put on a fresh pair of socks. "I suppose so. Yes."

"Right then. We're agreed we're leaving. I'm going to pack my rucksack. You should pack one too. Wherever we're going, whatever we're doing, we will never be coming back here.".

2

Wren placed her empty·rucksack on the bed. This was going to be tough. She stood in front of her trophy shelves. All the medals, all the prizes. As much as she would like to take them all with her, she could not. They were not practical. The rucksack would have to be filled with the essentials. "Maybe just one thing." She smiled and reached for an envelope on the back shelf. It was the letter saying she had been chosen to be a part of the team at the next Commonwealth games. She might not be able to fit in any of the Heptathlon trophies, but fitting in a letter was no big deal. She put it in a small plastic bag to make sure, even if it got wet, it would be safe, then she put it in the bottom of her rucksack.

"It's just a piece of paper y'know?" Robyn said as she watched from the doorway.

Wren flushed red. "I know," she mumbled.

"I'm only joking," replied Robyn, walking into the bedroom. "Mum and Dad were so proud the day that letter arrived."

"Thanks Robyn, that's really nice of you to say. Did you want something?"

"Naa, I'd just come to see what you were packing. I mean, it's a tough one isn't it? I want to take some photos, too. Of Mum...and Dad...and all of us." Wren started to cry again and Robyn hugged her. Tears began to roll down her cheeks too. All this had just happened; they were both still in shock, but they were forced to think about their own survival as well.

They stayed that way for a few moments before a scream from outside sent chills through them. They went to the window, staying to the side, making sure they could not be seen from the street. A woman was lying in the middle of the road; her arms flailed weakly as two creatures bit chunks out of her thighs and torso.

"Oh my god, that's Jessica's mum," Robyn said as the woman convulsed on the ground.

"And that's Jessica," Wren said, as one of the beasts pulled its mouth back from its victim. A chunk of bloody, spongy flesh dripped over its pallid chin as it ate in the bright afternoon sunshine. The two of them moved back from the window in fear of being seen. Both had the same look of horror on their faces. "I don't want to end up like that."

Robyn turned Wren around to face her. "Neither of us will."

"I think we should stay here the night, get everything prepared, and head out at first light tomorrow."

Robyn looked out of the window. "There's still plenty of daylight left."

"I know, but if we run into any problems and get stuck, we could still be in the city limits by nightfall, and that's something I don't want to risk."

"Good point," Robyn nodded.

"Have you thought about weapons?"

"Wren, how long have we been sisters? I haven't even thought about how I'm going to manage without Spotify. What kind of weapons were you thinking of?"

"Well, we need something practical. Dad's got loads of tools, and there's some stuff in the shed, but we shouldn't try to take anything that's too heavy. He's got a decent crowbar in the car…but something longer would be better. I don't really want to have to get too close to one of those things," Wren said.

"You've thought all this out, haven't you," Robyn said, flopping down on the bed. A sad look had come over her face, and the previous good humour was gone.

Wren sat down, placing her arm around her sister's shoulder. "I've always been this way. Coach told me that…I forget the exact quote, but it's something like 'every battle's won before it's fought.'"

"That's dumb."

"It's not really, Bobbi. Not when you think about it."

"It is. How does that make sense? I always thought that coach of yours was an arse."

"He wasn't. He was a good coach. A bit of a perv, but a good coach," Wren smiled.

"A perv? Did he try anything?" Robyn asked, turning towards Wren and becoming the older sister once more.

Wren laughed. "Erm, no, don't be daft."

"Hey, I've told you before. You're good looking. All my male friends think so. You shouldn't be hard on yourself."

"No, I don't mean because of that." Wren placed her hands over her breasts. "He might have been interested…if I didn't have these, and I had something else down there rather than what I've got. You understand now?" Wren asked, smiling.

Robyn laughed, "Yeah, now I get it."

"How the hell did we get onto Coach Chaplin's perving, anyway?"

"Something about fought battles, I dunno, I wasn't really listening.."

"Yeah. What it means is, planning is everything. We try and anticipate what we'll need to do, what we'll need to fight. That'll give us our best chance for surviving."

"I think he said it came from that book, *The Art of War*. Y'know, the Sun Tzu one?"

"Y'see, little sister. This is why you've never had a boyfriend," Robyn said, smiling.

"Better than being the school bike," Wren said, breaking into a wide grin.

"You cheeky little bitch," Robyn growled, pretending to strangle her. They both laughed for longer than the joke deserved.

"Are you okay?" Wren asked.

"It doesn't feel right to laugh."

"I was thinking the same, but I read somewhere it's actually very common after a trauma. Humour is an excellent coping mechanism."

"You are such a nerdtard."

"Hey, so I read. Sue me. I'm proud that I can sit down with a book that doesn't involve joining dots or finding Waldo."

"Bitch."

"Cow."

"Nerd."

"Slapper." They started to giggle again. "Come on, we'd better get packed."

Within half an hour, Wren's rucksack was ready to burst, packed with everything she could think of taking for any eventuality. "Bloody hell. What have you got in there?" Robyn asked, trying to lift the backpack off the bed, but struggling.

"I got the little camp stove that we used to use when we went to the shore. Food from downstairs, a couple of bottles of water, too. I left another two bottles down there for you to carry. I've got some batteries, a small torch, Swiss Army Knife—"

"Okay, okay! I was just saying it's flipping heavy. I didn't actually want a frikkin' list. God, what is it with you?"

"Are you packed?"

"Yep, all ready for tomorrow," Robyn said, throwing her rucksack down on the bed next to Wren's.

Wren looked at it for a moment. "Erm, what exactly have you got in there?"

"Everything I'll need."

"It looks a bit light…" Wren opened it up. "You've got socks, knickers, t-shirts, tampons, a spare pair of jeans…you are kidding me, Bobbi. We're not off on holiday! What is wrong with you? A frikkin' Rebecca Minkoff shoulder bag. How the hell is that going to help you?"

"I saved forever to get that. I used birthday and Christmas money. It's my single most prized possession. You took your envelope; I don't have anything that small."

Wren shook her head. "You said it yourself— prized possession. I didn't pack that letter because of what it was, I packed it because of what it meant. It is a reminder and a memento of all the hard work I put in. All the things I hoped for in my life. This…" Wren said, holding up the smooth, beige leather bag, "is just a thing. It has no practical purpose for what we're about to do."

"You're wrong. That bag was something I worked hard for; it was something I really wanted. I went without lots of things to get that bag. I saved and saved and saved. I've never done that before. I always spent money on clothes and make-up as soon as I got it, but not with that bag. I'm not saying it's as important as your accomplishments, Wren, I'm not an idiot. But I proved something to myself with that bag. I proved that I could be self-disciplined…you wouldn't understand, it all comes so easily to you," Robyn said sadly.

"Nothing came easily. I had to work for everything. I was out training in all-weather while you were still in bed. I would go to school, train all afternoon, then do my homework. I had zero social life; books ended up being my only friends because I knew what I wanted to do. I focussed on my goal, and look what I missed out on. The world's gone and I never got to experience most of it. So, don't tell me I wouldn't understand about sacrifice," Wren said, throwing the bag down onto the bed.

"I didn't mean it like that…. Look, it doesn't matter anyway. You're right, I suppose," Robyn said, letting out a long sigh. "I did really love that bag."

Wren looked at her sister, then looked back down at the bag. "No, I get it. I'm sorry…. How about this…?" Wren picked up the bag and unhooked the four colour shoulder strap. "Pink, red, white and blue? bleugh!!!" She smiled and carefully hooked and wrapped the designer strap around one of the shoulder harnesses on the rucksack. She held it up to show Robyn. "See, we've both got reminders now."

Robyn smiled. "Thank you," she said, more than a little embarrassed.

"Come on, let's get this rucksack packed properly."

3

The next morning, Wren was awake at first light. She had set the alarm on her watch to take care of the final preparations before heading out. She had not slept much, as the sounds of the dying city around her kept bleeding into her dreams, but she had survived on less. She headed down the hallway to the bathroom, filled the sink and threw plenty of cold water over her face before washing with soap. She knew it would not be long before the water stopped running too, and she wondered if this would be the last ever time she enjoyed the luxury.

Wren headed back down the hallway and into her sister's room. "Bobbi...Bobbi," she said, gently shaking her sister's shoulder in an effort to rouse her.

Robyn let out a small whine and turned over. "Five more minutes," she said, her face pressing into the pillow."

"No...now," Wren replied, whipping the warm quilt off her in one movement.

"What the fuck???" Robyn shouted, jumping out of bed and facing up to Wren. "Don't you dare do that to me!"

Wren stepped back a little. "Hey. We need to go. This is an important day. I told you we needed an early start. I'm going to go make us breakfast, then we're getting our stuff together and we're out of here. Get over yourself, princess."

Robyn's lip curled into something approaching a snarl. "Get out of my room now!"

Wren turned and left. As she walked back along the landing, a self-satisfied smile swept across her face. She went down the stairs and stepped into the kitchen, and suddenly, the smile disappeared.

The light from the windows vanished. There stood her mum, crying. It was the night of the Prime Minister's address. The one that changed everything. The one that had told them practically every country, all over the world, had fallen victim to this reanimating virus. People died and then they got up again, but not like they were before. They turned into these killing machines that were only interested in eating the flesh of the living and spreading the virus.

Internet and mobile coverage had been really bad for months before. Cyber-attacks had crippled the world's communications, and just when they thought it was sorted, another would hit, then another. It had not just been limited to communications. The power grid had been affected; in fact, most things had been affected. Some thought it was the Russians. Some thought it was the Chinese. Some thought it was the North Koreans. Some thought it was Islamic fundamentalists. Nobody really knew, and it was difficult to find blame. These attacks were on a global scale. The world had been struggling long before the Prime Minister's speech, but the day before, during one of the spells of broken internet coverage, Wren remembered seeing some footage on YouTube of someone being pounced on by one of the reanimated corpses. It was horrific and bloody as the creature had sunk its teeth into the neck of its victim. The bitten woman had fallen, clutching her wound, before her arm fell limply to her side and she lay still. Within a few seconds, the woman was back on her feet, but not like before. Now there was a cheetah-like spring in her step. Now she was something else.

When Wren had seen the clip, she thought it was part of an elaborate hoax, as did everybody else. More of them appeared online, but still, it seemed like the latest internet prank, a fake news Ice Bucket Challenge, or the Ten-Year Challenge. This was the Zombie Challenge—create the scariest, most lifelike zombie attack video you can and pass it on. The internet was patchy again for the rest of the day, but most of the kids were talking about it in school. The following day, the internet was haywire again, but when the Prime Minister's broadcast came on in the evening, Wren knew all the videos had been real. The world *had* in fact gone to hell.

Wren had hugged and held her mum, but she was inconsolable. She had said, "All any parent wants is for their children to grow up in a better world than they did. Now there might not be a world at all."

A *thud* from upstairs dragged Wren back from her reminiscing. Most memories in this house were happy ones; she would be sorry to leave them behind, but there were some, like this one, she would be grateful never to be reminded of again. She made peanut butter sandwiches for their breakfast, and, looking at the remaining half loaf, decided to make peanut butter sandwiches with the rest of it, too. That would be their lunch when they stopped.

Wren had packed some dried packets of couscous and some noodles. They were lighter than cans. She had also put a small saucepan in her rucksack; she knew Robyn would not even have thought of anything like that.

Eventually, her sister joined her. "I need a coffee," she said grumpily as she walked into the kitchen.

"I can make you an iced coffee, minus the ice."

Robyn put her middle finger up and slumped onto the stool at the breakfast bar, crossing her arms on the marble effect surface and placing her forehead down on them. "It's so early. The last time I got up at this time was when we went on holiday to Spain, three years ago."

"Stop moaning and eat your breakfast," replied Wren, sliding the plate and a glass of water over to her. "I forgot how much fun you were in the morning."

Robyn brought her head up from the counter and extended her middle finger again. The two of them ate and drank in silence for a while. "Have you looked outside?"

"Yeah. It looks like it's going to be a nice day. At least we're not going to get rained on," Wren replied.

"I didn't mean that. I mean…it looks like any other day out there. There's no sign of anything out of the ordinary."

"Other than a pool of blood in the centre of the road and a van on its side in one of our neighbour's living rooms."

"Well, yeah, smart arse, but you know what I mean."

"Yeah, I do. I expected to see the street swimming with those things."

"Maybe it's not as bad as we think. Maybe it's being brought under control. I heard a lot of gunshots earlier on last night, did you?"

"Yeah. You'd hope they'd bring the army in to help save the Scottish capital, wouldn't you?" Wren said.

"Problem is, the gunfire didn't last for long, did it?"

"I know." The two of them went back to eating in silence for a while. "I want to go to the school."

"What? Why would you want to go back there? If there is something good to come about from this whole end of the world thing, it's that we never have to go back to that dump."

"I've been thinking about weapons," Wren replied. "I've packed us a crowbar, a couple of knives, a couple of long screwdrivers, but I was thinking about some of the stuff there. I think getting us a couple of javelins would be a really good idea." She finished off her sandwich and put the plate in the bowl.

"You are mental if you think I'm going back to that place just to break into the sports equipment shed."

"Think about it, Robyn. They're over two metres long. If we come into contact with any of those things out there, do you want them to be close enough to bite you while you stick a knife in their face? Or do you want a two-metre gap while you spear them with a big metal spear?"

Robyn took the final bite from her sandwich and pushed the plate over the countertop towards Wren. "Two metres back, I suppose, but if I have to face any of those things, I don't rate my chances. I'm not the sporty type like you. I don't have a lot of strength in my arms."

"Muscle can be built, technique can be learned. You've just got to have the right attitude," Wren said, taking her sister's plate and placing it in the washing up bowl on top of her own. "Get your stuff together. We'll head out in five."

"Yes Commandant," Robyn replied.

Wren took one final look around the house while Robyn was getting ready. Was there anything else there that was portable and could help them? No. She had got everything the pair of them could physically carry that would be of any use. She heard feet coming down the stairs and went out into the hallway to meet her sister.

"Ready?" Robyn asked.

"You are not seriously heading out in that?"

"What? What's wrong with it?"

"For a start, your jacket's not waterproof, your jeans have got tears in them and you won't get a mile in those boots without complaining your feet hurt. You should be wearing this kind of stuff," said Wren gesturing to her own outfit.

"Erm, what? The smelly hiker outfit? It's going to be a sunny day. You said yourself. I don't want to be wearing heavy stuff; I'll sweat."

"At least find yourself a waterproof jacket, and change those boots to something more practical. We're going to be covering over a hundred and fifty miles, a lot of it will be cross country."

"Oh I tell you what, why don't you just come upstairs and pick my outfit for me?"

"Why do you have to be like this? I'm trying to help."

"No, you're trying to boss me around. You're my younger sister. I don't take orders from you." Something approaching rage bled onto Robyn's face, and Wren let out a long sigh.

"Fine. Do what you want, but when you can't walk in those boots anymore, I'm leaving you behind. You can make your own way to Grandad's place."

Robyn thought about saying something back for a moment, but just puffed and flared her nostrils before stomping back up the stairs. Wren waited, adjusting the strap on her rucksack, and practising some movements just to gauge how much physical freedom she had carrying something so heavy. It was a few minutes before Robyn came back down the stairs.

"There," she said, gesturing towards her leather jacket, leather trousers and trainers. "Happy now, dork?"

Wren shook her head. "It doesn't matter what it looks like. All that matters now is practicality."

"Whatever," replied Robyn, picking up her rucksack. "What the f—" she said, as the strain of the weight took her off guard. "What have you put in my rucksack? I'm not carrying that weight. Give me yours, I'll carry that," she said, gesturing for Wren to hand the other rucksack over to her. Wren smiled and did as she was asked. Robyn stumbled forward and the rucksack fell to the floor. "What have you got in these? Jesus!"

"I've got the things we're going to need, Robyn. We don't know what's going to happen; we need to make sure we're prepared. They'll get lighter as time goes on.

There's food in them. Over time, I'll figure out about catching our own food and stuff, but right now, what we've got in our rucksacks could be the difference between living and dying."

"Gross. Catching our own food. You think you're that guy Tom Hanks played? Who was it? Robinson Crusoe. You think you're him? We're not on a desert island y'know."

"I don't even know where to begin with putting right what you just said," Wren said, picking her rucksack back up and placing it over her shoulders. She walked straight past Robyn and unlocked the back door. "Are you ready?"

"Why are we going out the back way?"

"Because we're heading to the school, and the fastest way is over the back fence, across McIntyre's field and through the park," replied Wren. "Unless you'd like to head out of the front door and walk through a big housing estate. I tell you what. You do that, and I'll meet you there in say," Wren looked at her watch, "Never."

"Fuuuccckkk yooouuu!!!"

Wren put her middle finger up before stepping out into the cool morning air.

Robyn stayed in the hall for a moment. This journey was going to be a nightmare. Butterflies were already flapping around in her stomach like they were caught in a twister, and she was taking orders from her nerdy little sister. She let out a long breath and began to follow her. "Wait for me," she said as she got outside and pulled the door to.

Wren whipped around angrily, "Shhh!" she said, gesturing for her to keep her voice low.

And so it begins, Robyn thought, as she followed Wren up the back garden path. The garden was enclosed with six-foot-high panel fencing, but the section to the right had sustained damage in the last heavy winds and several of the slats had blown off or shifted position, meaning they could see their neighbour's garden and vice versa. Thankfully, at five twenty-five a.m., there was not much to see. They got to the end of the path and Wren took off her rucksack. It took a couple of goes, but she eventually summoned the strength to push it up, then over the fence. It thudded as it hit the long grass on the other side. She gestured for Robyn to hand her the other rucksack, and managed to get that one over with greater ease.

"You go first."

"Okay," Wren replied, grabbing hold of the top of the tall fencing and pulling herself up deftly before placing one hiking boot on top and jumping down the other side.

The main reason Robyn had wanted her sister to go first was to see how she did it. Having watched her, she was less confident than ever. She grabbed the top of the fence and jumped up; her feet immediately swung inwards, smashing through one of the panels and getting stuck. She lost her grip on the top of the fence and, like a huge pendulum, fell back. She landed with a thump on her dad's vegetable patch. Robyn looked towards her feet as they dangled through the broken panel of the fence. She almost screamed when Wren's face came into view. It was contorted with fits of laughter.

"Don't laugh! Help me!" demanded Robyn, as loudly as she dared. She tried to wiggle her feet loose, but the panel was sharp and she did not want to risk cutting herself. "Help me," she said again.

When Wren finally brought her laughter under control, she knelt down. Now the structure of the fence was weakened, she removed five horizontal panels, not just freeing Robyn's feet, but making a gap big enough for her to crawl through. "Come on," she said, gesturing for her sister to climb through.

Robyn refused to speak for some time after that. They crossed the field and got through the park with no effort at all. They did not see a single person or creature, other than birds and squirrels. For the rest of nature, life was going on as normal. There was a new apex predator, but nothing that would bother them; in fact, it would probably help them. Wren remembered watching a documentary about what would happen to cities if humans died out. Nobody ever thought it could possibly happen, but now it looked like it was a fairly safe bet. In the programme, the cities gradually gave way to nature once more. Creeping vines grew around buildings, weeds cracked through roads and pavements and over years and decades, nature reclaimed huge swathes of industrialised land. So, now, as she looked at the squirrels and the birds whose habitat had become steadily smaller and more toxic by the year, she wondered if in fact there were some winners in this thing.

"Okay, stop," Wren said crouching down and signalling for Robyn to do the same. They were behind a thick growth of shrubbery near the main entrance to the park. Across the road was a huge recreation ground known as the Rec, with a football pitch, a rugby pitch, an all-weather pitch and a makeshift athletics track that Wren had trained on many times. To the right and left of the huge sports field were houses, and at the far end were changing and equipment rooms. Beyond those was the beginning of the school complex.

"So, we just hop over the road then cross that massive open expanse that's right in the middle of two big housing estates. Great idea...not!"

"It's not ideal, but see how you feel when we come face to face with one of those things and all you've got is a screwdriver and a knife...y'know what, in fact, screw it. I'm already sick to death of you. You stay here," Wren said, slipping off her rucksack and peeling off her jacket, revealing a black vest. She pulled out the crowbar from the side of her pack and opened up a small pouch, taking out a Swiss army knife, which she placed in her pocket.

"What? What the hell do you think you're doing?" Robyn demanded.

"I'm not putting up with your Prima Donna shit anymore. You want to come up with the ideas, come up with the ideas, but this is the best plan we've got. Stay here with the rucksacks. If you see anything, run...or climb a tree, I don't care. I'm going to get what we came here for."

"Hey!" Robyn said, beginning to stand, but it was already too late.

Wren began to sprint towards the park entrance. She was across the road and moving down the centre of the Rec before Robyn had managed to shuffle out of the straps of her rucksack. For a split second, she forgot why they were there and was about to shout after her younger sister. But then she caught herself and ducked down again. "I'm going to murder the little bitch," she muttered to herself. Robyn looked around the park; it was only small compared to some the city had, but it was too big to be exposed like she was. She shoved both rucksacks under the shrubbery and kept down, only occasionally pricking her head up to do a quick scan of the area. "Damn you, Wren."

Wren could not keep sprinting speed up for long; she just wanted to make sure there was no way her sister had a hope of running after her. She continued at a steadier pace down the centre of the track, looking from side to side at the surrounding houses. How many times had footballs or rugby balls ended up in these back gardens? As exposed as it was, and it *was* exposed, she was not overly concerned about being seen. It was before six a.m. and it would be the streets and front gardens that were the danger zone. Whatever else the zombies were, they did not strike her as big horticulturists.

Wren slowed down as she approached the changing room and equipment shed. The wooden door to the boys changing room had been smashed in. She came to a stop and turned three hundred and sixty degrees, making sure there was no movement, making sure she had not caught the attention of one of those beasts. It was all clear, and the sun continued to rise, making the dew glisten magically. She turned her attention back to the changing room and took a deep breath before taking the crowbar in her right hand. She swung it around a little, getting a feel for the weight of it before stepping into the dim interior.

She had been in the girl's changing room a thousand times, maybe even more, but had never ventured onto this side of the building. The layout was exactly the same. A large Perspex skylight allowed the early morning sun to wander in. Without even realising, she had been holding her breath walking through the door, but now, as no zombies came hurtling towards her, she let out a long breath. She nearly gagged as she breathed in again as the smell of urine overcame her. "Eugh! Gross!" she said, as she walked around the corner to the shower area. The smell became even stronger as the open shower had obviously been used as a toilet by vandals. Spray paint decorated the walls with the names of teachers and pupils. Who was fit, who wanted to do what to who, who needed a good this, who needed a good that. "Simpletons," she spat, before heading back out and taking a deep breath of fresh morning air.

Wren walked around the back of the building to the girls' changing room. The door was intact, but she felt no urge to go in. She remembered the stale, mildewy smell without stepping foot any closer. The equipment shed was a brick annexe next to the entrance to the girls' changing room. Wren paused for a moment and looked left, beyond the edge of the Rec, and down the slope to the school grounds. She'd never been a fan of the school. She did not like the building, nor did she care for the teachers particularly. She hardly had any friends because of her rigorous training schedule, but in fairness, even if she hadn't been so involved in training, it was unlikely she would have had many. She was not a sociable type; she was not a team player. She had always been a loner. That's why she ran track instead of joining a team sport. But the one thing that she knew she would miss about the place was learning.

Despite her lonely state, school brought her happiness because she could fill her head with knowledge. She would miss that; she would miss...she would miss Mairi Baker, the head librarian. The school building was attached to the local public library and to most, Miss Baker was a crotchety old spinster who disliked people, disliked children even more—but loved books. For some reason, she'd taken a real shine to Wren; she saw a kindred spirit in her. One of Wren's proudest moments was when Miss Baker, who never got involved in any school or community activities, actually travelled to see Wren in an athletics competition. Yes, she would miss Mairi Baker. She hoped she was safe, and if she was not, she hoped that she did not suffer.

Wren jerked out of her daydream and turned back towards the red-painted wooden door. None of the equipment within was modern; all the expensive items were kept down at the gymnasium, so a lock and a padlock were sufficient deterrents. Wren fed the crowbar through the hasp of the padlock and began to pull hard. The wood underneath chipped and then there was the sound of splitting wood as the screw plate snapped, falling to the cement steps along with the padlock. Wren carefully placed the straight edge of the crowbar in the small gap between the door and the door frame, just above the lock. She levered it from side to side, breaking wood on both the door and the frame, allowing her to get the bar in even deeper. She continued until she felt the lock itself begin to give. She dug the crowbar in deeper still, then pulled with all her strength. There was an ear-splitting crack, and the door flew open, revealing a bounty of footballs, hockey sticks, rounders bats, shots, discuses and there, right at the back, javelins. Wren climbed over the other equipment and grabbed two of the newest looking ones. She stumbled back out of the equipment shed and leant them against a wall before she reached back inside for one of the hockey sticks.

Wren stepped off the paving slabs surrounding the brick building, and onto the grass. She had played hockey a couple of times, but it was not for her. She liked the game, but the whole team thing…being told what to do had never suited her that much. She regarded the hockey stick as she held it up in her hands. She gauged the weight like she had done with the crowbar earlier. It felt good. It felt like it would also make a decent weapon if she was in a tight spot. Maybe she would take this for herself and the javelin for Robyn. She continued to swing, left and right, and a smile crept onto her face as confidence grew with this newfound weapon. She loved the whooshing sound it made as it swept through the cool morning air. It gave her a real feeling of power. *Whoosh! Whoosh! Whoosh!* Then suddenly, she heard something else…a growling sound. She stumbled back onto the paving slabs and her back hit the brick wall of the building as she tried to zero in on the source of the sound. The growl got louder and her head whisked from side to side; she could feel her body tense and she looked down at her knuckles as they turned white around the hockey stick handle. She caught movement out of the corner of her eye and let out a breath of relief as she saw a dog's tail, then its hindquarters, then the dog's head.

"Hello there, boy," she said, crouching down, but the dog ignored her. He continued to growl. She moved towards him; he cast a quick glance in her direction then turned around and began to run full speed down the hill towards the school. Wren edged towards the corner of the building and remained there for a few seconds before casting a glance around the side. One of the reanimated creatures was about thirty metres back. For the time being it was not looking in her direction, but there was no way she could get back to the park without passing it.

She brought her head back around quickly and rested it against the cold brick. Wren looked towards the broken door. *Had the noise attracted it?* She looked at the hockey stick again, then back down at the javelins. They had a much longer reach, and now she was so close to one of those things again, the bravado had left her. *The longer reach the better*, she thought. She placed the stick down and reached for the two javelins. Weight was not an issue; at just eight hundred grams each, it was not an exertion for Wren to carry two of them, but they were cumbersome. No, it would be stupid to try and outrun the creature while carrying two javelins, which left just one option. She could feel the adrenaline begin to surge through her system. She put one of the javelins against the wall and walked with the other to the edge of the changing room building once again. She put her head around the corner, but now there was no sign of the creature she had seen. She edged out a little farther, but still, there was nothing. Slowly she walked along the side of the building, holding the javelin out in front of her like a mediaeval pike-man. She reached the front and drew the javelin back in as she peeked her head around the corner. Nothing. *Maybe he's gone into the open changing room.* Maybe she could make a run for it without the creature being any the wiser.

Wren quickly headed back round to grab the other javelin. She was almost running by the time she reached the corner, and that's when she came face to face with it. Although she had witnessed her dad turn and her mum get bitten, she had never seen one of these creatures head-on. Her mouth dropped open and she forgot how to breathe in that instant. Terror gripped her in its icy tendrils; she could feel her heart expand and contract, expand and contract, as suddenly her body needed more oxygen than ever. Eventually, she inhaled a quaking gasp of air, and her own sound jolted her out of the split-second freeze-frame.

The creature let out a fearsome growl as it jerked forward to run the few feet between itself and Wren. In life it had been a shop assistant; it still wore the uniform, albeit tattered and bloody. The pallid complexion was a shade lighter than the filmy grey eyes, but it was the jet pupils that entranced Wren as the creature beat a path towards her. Like a drop of black paint on white—a shattered ink drop on glistening snow, they flared, sending shivers through every fibre of her body.

By accident more than deliberate action, the javelin speared the beast in the stomach, somehow finding the spine. Wren felt something crack, and the beast collapsed to the ground, coming to rest on its side. Still it tried to drag itself towards its new-found prey. Wren backed away and the creature continued to claw and slither across the pavement and grass towards her dragging the javelin along, growling and gurgling as it moved.

Wren walked backwards, watching it every step of the way. It continued to follow her. She guessed its spinal column had been severed, as the beast's legs now seemed completely immobile, but that did nothing to halt its resolve. She headed around the side of the building and continued to reverse slowly. Fear still possessed her, and as she saw the grey fingers of the creature emerge from around the corner, another in a long line of shivers ran down her spine. The beast looked almost comical as it tried to move with the long skewer protruding from its stomach, but the comedy was lost on Wren for the time being as she watched the beast bare its teeth and thick globules of saliva dribble from its mouth.

When she had led it two metres down the side of the building, she turned and ran, blocking out the gurgling growls and the scraping sound of the javelin against the paving slabs as best she could. She turned the corner, ran, turned again, ran and turned again. She was back at the equipment shed. Wren climbed back in and grabbed another javelin before reaching for the one she had leant against the wall. She had no desire to see that creature one last time. It was useless now; it would live out the rest of its days a crawling, struggling monstrosity, but it could not harm her anymore.

She did not look back to the changing rooms for old time's sake as she ran across the field towards the park. She sang a little song in her head until she was far enough away not to hear the growls and the scraping. A tear ran down her face. Over one hundred and fifty miles to travel; she had barely got out of her front yard and she had almost died. Sadness overcame her, and the first tear was joined by another, then another. This really was the end of everything.

4

Wren slowed down as she reached the end of the Rec. She did not want her sister to see that she had been crying. As much as Robyn angered and irritated her, she did not want to share her fear. She did not have Wren's resolve, and to fuel her negativity at the beginning of such a long trek would be counter-productive. They had to make this journey, no matter what, so why make it harder on herself?

Wren looked at her watch; it was just past six o'clock. Normally at this time, some people would be making their trip to work. The newsagents would be opening. Taxis and buses would be breaking the early morning quiet, pumping the first of their blue/grey exhaust fumes into the cool air. Wren knew this because she often saw the city waking up. She had usually been training for an hour or thereabouts when the suburbs began to ripple with life.

She wiped the last of her tears away, took a deep breath and ran across the road, careful not to let either of the javelins drag on the ground and make noise. Her heart began to race again when she looked towards the spot she had left Robyn and could see no sign of her, but as she got closer, she saw a figure crouched down by the thick growth of shrubs.

Wren placed the javelins down on the ground and walked up to Robyn, who stood up and immediately slapped her younger sister across the face. "Never do that to me again."

It was more shock than pain that rendered Wren silent, and her mouth dropped open, lost for words, while her hand went up to her cheek. She almost snarled as her hand flew through the air and slapped Robyn, who let out a small shriek. Wren immediately realised the foolishness of what they were doing and gestured with her hands for Robyn to calm down. It was too late though, and Robyn leapt towards her sister, grabbing her by her jacket. She brought her hand up again, ready to hit her, but Wren took a tight hold of Robyn's upper arms, extended her right leg behind her sister's and pushed. Robyn fell with her arms still flailing. She landed heavily on the dew-soaked grass, and let out another, louder shriek. Wren leapt on top of her, pinning her hands and arms to the ground. "Shut up!" she hissed. "Something will hear us."

"Get off me. Get off me now, you little shit!"

"I said, keep your mouth shut. Otherwise, I swear, I will leave you here. I'll make my own way to Inverness."

Something changed in Robyn's eyes, and suddenly, the fight left her. She went limp beneath Wren, and feeling this, Wren released her and climbed to her feet, offering her sister a hand.

Robyn ignored it and struggled to her feet, wiping the dew from her leather trousers. "I hate you. I wish it was you who'd been bitten instead of Mum and Dad." Robyn struggled with her rucksack, but eventually got it onto her shoulders, then turned to walk off.

Wren just stood there watching her. "Hey!" Robyn did not reply, she just carried on walking. "Hey, bitch! Don't forget your javelin. Your breath might kill humans, I don't know if it will work on those things."

Robyn stopped. She looked down at the javelins and without looking back, or acknowledging Wren in any way, picked one up and carried on walking.

"You're welcome," Wren said to herself before swinging her own rucksack onto her back and collecting the other javelin. She caught up to her sister and put her hand on Robyn's shoulder. There were tears in her sister's eyes. Up until this moment, Wren had not realised she had actually applied a small amount of mascara and it had run. She could not help it; the sight of it made her laugh, and Robyn began to cry even more. She dropped the javelin and slumped to the ground, crossing her legs and holding her head in her hands like a small child.

Wren knelt down in front of her. "Leave me if you want to leave me," Robyn said. Wren reached out and gently dabbed the black streaks away with her thumb. They did not disappear, but they were better than they were, and the action itself was an act of conciliation.

"We have to stick together. It's the only way we stand a chance."

"Why? What good am I?"

"Listen, these things are quick. If we get stuck in a tight spot and we have to run, I'm a lot faster than you, so you'll be a good diversion while I get away."

Robyn began to laugh through the last of her tears. "Bitch!"

"Takes one to know one."

"I'm sorry for what I said. That was horrible."

"You didn't mean it."

"No, I did, I just shouldn't have said it to your face."

"Bitch," Wren said, beginning to giggle.

"Takes one to know one."

Wren stood up and offered a hand to her sister, who took it this time. They both picked up their weapons and continued their journey. Rather than leaving the park, they continued to the north wall, which bordered a large wooded area. Wren threw her rucksack over the six-foot, red brick divide, followed by Robyn's rucksack and the two javelins. She looked at Robyn. "Jump, get a grip on the top, and then I'll help push you up."

Robyn, looked a little embarrassed that she needed help. "Okay…." She frowned, jumped, caught hold of the top, and her feet began to flail against the side of the wall.

"Stop kicking!" Wren growled.

Robyn felt Wren's hands shove her buttocks hard. "*Aaarghhh!*" The shove took her by surprise, but she managed to mount the top of the wall before clumsily lowering herself on the other side. "*Aaarghhh!*" she screamed again.

"Keep your voice down," hissed Wren.

"Wren! *Help!*" This scream was not one of getting caught on a branch or landing awkwardly. This scream was something much more.

Wren did not miss a beat. She jumped up and vaulted the wall, landing neatly on the other side, immediately seeing the creature running up the weed covered embankment towards them. The javelins had slid down the incline, the rucksacks half-way down. Wren pulled out the straight edge screwdriver from the back of her jeans and held it in front of herself, ready. She caught movement out of the corner of her eye as Robyn bent down to pick up a heavy branch.

The clumsy creature stumbled twice, but the malevolence and intent never left its face as its eyes fixed on the two girls. At the top of the embankment, they had the advantage of height, and the second it came within distance, Wren kicked out hard, making contact with it square in the chest. Almost in slow motion, it toppled backwards, reverse somersaulting down the hill in a cascading jumble of arms and legs. Wren wasted no time, running down the hill after it. In one swooping movement, she grabbed a javelin and, as the writhing body of the beast came to a stop on the flat ground at the bottom of the hill, Wren drove the javelin straight through its heart with all her strength. She felt it go through. She felt it dig deep into the earth on the other side. The creature remained pinned there, desperately reaching towards her, but unable to move. She stepped back just in case and looked up to the top of the embankment where her sister still stood, frozen in terror.

Wren was hypnotised as she watched it struggle like a giant beetle caught on its back, trying to right itself. "The head," called Robyn, as she broke her pose and slowly began to negotiate the wooded embankment.

"What?"

"I heard someone say at school that their dad's brother had been down in Portsmouth when they had the outbreak. They were in the army and they had been told that the only way to kill them was to shoot them in the head.

"That's handy. Got a gun?"

"Well, y'know, anything in the head. A bullet...a spear...big rock?"

Wren walked over to the other javelin, picked it up and handed it to Robyn. "Be my guest."

The pair of them looked down at the struggling beast. They looked at its ferocious eyes and snarling mouth, baring dirty yellow teeth. It wore filthy jeans, a beige pullover that looked two sizes too big; a threadbare coat and trainers with one hole in the toe. He was most certainly a street dweller, in life, who had probably camped somewhere within the grove. Now, he had joined the multitudes who were no longer divided by social position. There were only two classes: alive, or dead.

"It smells terrible," Robyn said as her eyes followed the beast's thrashing hands.

Both girls stood there in morbid fascination. Then the beast began to jerk even harder and the javelin slowly started moving, in a greater arc. Robyn and Wren jumped back. The more the javelin loosened in the ground, the more agitated the creature became, and the more it wriggled and writhed until finally, the soft earth gave way, and it rolled onto its side. The javelin whipped down and both girls jumped back farther to get out of its way.

The beast scrambled to its feet with the javelin still sticking out of its back. Wren looked across at Robyn, who was just stood there, her mouth agog, staring. "Kill it!" Wren shouted.

The beast headed towards them, and Robyn just watched in horror as it lunged for Wren. Wren grabbed the end of the Javelin, but the creature kept advancing, sliding its body further onto the shaft, like some rancid piece of meat slopping down a skewer. She felt scared, revulsed and physically sick all at the same time as the growls, the smell and the monstrous sight hammered her senses like a battering ram of toxic sludge.

Each second, the creature's grabbing hands moved closer. She glanced towards Robyn, but she was still paralysed with fear. Realising she had to do something or she would be joining the ranks of the dead herself, she extended her foot once more and booted the creature hard. It shot backwards, losing its footing and sliding right off the end of the javelin before falling into a heap on the ground. It scrambled to its feet once more and ran towards Wren again. It was too close for her to stab it with the end of the long javelin, so instead, she battered the side of its head, using the javelin like a Bojutsu staff. The creature did not lose its footing, but veered off course, stumbling past Wren, before it regained its balance. It turned again and lurched for her once more, but this time, she was not encumbered by the large oak tree at her back and she thrust the point of the javelin in the direction of the creature's head, closing her eyes and turning away at the same time. She felt something dense and heard a popping sound, then the growls came to an instant stop and a dead weight on the end of the javelin ripped it out of her hands as it dropped. She opened her eyes and looked towards her sister who was stood, mouth gaping for a half-second before a jet of semi-digested food jettisoned from it.

Eventually, Wren turned her head around to look towards the creature. The bloody end of the javelin had slipped out as it collapsed to the ground. She looked in the general direction of its face, but she already felt queasy, and seeing anything in graphic detail would not help her in any way, so she cleaned off the end of the javelin on the beast's clothes and went to collect their rucksacks while Robyn threw up a second time.

"Are you okay?" Wren asked, gently rubbing her sister's back after placing the rucksack down beside her.

"Are you trying to be funny?" She was bent over and had her hands on her knees. Her eyes were red with retching, but nothing was coming out.

"I mean, y'know."

"I'll live. Well for the next few minutes anyway," she said, wiping her mouth and standing up straight. "That's the grossest thing I've ever seen in my entire life."

"Stop looking at it then."

Robyn went across to pick up the other javelin, slid her own rucksack onto her shoulders and kicked some dirt and twigs over where she'd been sick, almost as if she was ashamed. The two sisters began walking again, each throwing glances back at the gruesome scene until they were finally out of sight.

"I don't know if I'll be able to do what you did," Robyn said.

"What do you mean?"

"I don't know if I'll be able to kill one of them. I nearly peed myself just watching you."

"Hey, it was luck. I held out the javelin in the direction, I closed my eyes and hoped for the best. I was just as scared as you."

"But that's the difference. I froze. You were scared, and you still managed to save us."

"Like I said. It was luck. The more of them we face, the easier it will get. It might be an idea for us to practice a little bit, though."

"Practice?"

"Yeah. I mean, nothing comes without practice. Even just the basics."

"No thanks. Next time, I think I'll just try not to freeze, and run like hell or climb a tree or something."

"Great," Wren replied. "That'll get us a long way."

5

The two of them slowed as they approached the end of the wooded area. Wren signalled for Robyn to crouch down, so they had cover in the shrubbery, long grass, and last remaining trees, while they looked over the road. There was an industrial estate. To the left and right was nothing but long stretches of concrete and cement. It was a vast trading estate bordered by council housing estates. To the north of the industrial estate was the start of miles of rolling fields of farmland. But to get through the trading estate meant they would have to abandon the shelter of the trees.

Wren looked at her watch. "It's seven-fifteen. All things considered, we've made pretty good time. Once we get through that bit, we're through to farmland."

"You make it sound easy."

"Well, I don't see anybody. Do you?"

"We might get lucky. We might not run into any of them. We deserve some luck, don't we?"

Robyn ignored the question. "So, what's the plan?"

"Do you think you can run with the rucksack on your back?"

"I can barely walk with it on my back."

"Okay, then we walk. If we run into anything, drop the rucksack so we can put up a fight, or run if we need to."

"What about all the supplies? You said we needed so much."

"Not going to do us much good if we're dead. If it comes to it, we can always find more supplies. We won't get a second chance if we come face to face with one of those things and it gets hold of us. Okay, do you need a drink? Do you need to pee? Because when we start this, we're not stopping until we're on the other side of that estate."

"Don't treat me like a child. I know when I need to pee, thanks very much."

"Okay, okay. Let's go," Wren said, stepping out from the safety of the woods.

"Wait! Wait, please," she said in a whisper.

"What is it?"

"I don't want to do this."

"No shit," Wren replied. "Do you think I do? But if we don't get across the fields, the only other option is going through housing estates."

"No. I mean, I want to go back home, Wren." Robyn flopped onto her behind and crossed her legs.

Wren stepped back through the shrubbery and crouched down. "We've been through this. Things are only going to get worse. We can't afford to be in a city the size of Edinburgh; it's suicide."

"Who are we fooling, Wren? I'm not going to be able to fight those things. I froze back there. You didn't, I did."

"I can't do this by myself. I can't get there by myself. I wouldn't want to."

"The army could get all this back under control. Maybe we should head back home, make it as secure as we can, and just wait it out."

"No. We're wasting time. We need to go now."

"Aren't you listening?"

"I hear you, but it's you who's not listening," Wren replied, dragging Robyn to her feet.

"Get off me...get off me," she protested, like an angry child.

"This is what's going to happen. We're heading out there now. If any of those things come and we can't outrun them, I'm going to deal with them. We're going to get to the other side, we're going to find somewhere quiet and safe, and then we're going to start training. You and me. We're going to start training together."

"What do you mean, training?" Robyn asked, with a puzzled look on her face.

"We're going to learn how to fight. Properly, I mean."

"How? What do either of us know about fighting?"

"Not much, but I know a lot about training, and the first thing you need to identify when you come up with a training plan are a list of objectives. You work back from there. I know we can become better equipped to deal with these things, I know it. Let's just get this next hurdle out of the way. Deal?"

Robyn looked across the road to the large industrial estate and let out a sigh. "Deal."

They made sure their rucksacks were comfortable on their shoulders, before collecting their javelins and setting off. Instinctively, they stayed low as they headed out of the thick shrubbery, almost as if they thought that would keep them hidden as they darted across the empty dual carriageway in front of them. Their heads shot from side to side, constantly checking the roads and pathways for any movement, but it was clear. They got to the other side and Wren signalled for Robyn to follow her over to the side of one of the large industrial buildings. There was a narrow path all the way around it, bordered by the odd bush. Nothing significant. But some cover was better than none.

They remained low as they skirted the building, Wren leading and looking back regularly to make sure Robyn was following. The screaming engine of a motorbike shot by on the dual carriageway, freezing them in their tracks. The almost deafening echoes ricocheted off the side of the buildings in the vast trading estate, and that's when they began to hear the ghoulish chorus of growls rise into the air around them.

"Ohhh shiiittt!" Wren said as the first of the creatures began to emerge up ahead. "Ruuunnn!"

"*Run where?!*" Robyn asked, panicking.

"Home. Back home," Wren replied, throwing the rucksack off her shoulders and shoving it underneath one of the leafy bushes. Robyn did the same, and the two of them began to sprint with their spears as fast as they could.

"I can't run that far," Robyn said.

Wren looked back as they darted across the dual carriageway. Dozens of creatures were pouring from the side streets of the industrial estate, originally roused by the sound of the racing bike, but now, transfixed by the figures sprinting away from them. "Don't look back. Whatever you do, don't look back."

Robyn immediately looked back. "Oh...my...God!" she said in between sucking in huge lungfuls of air. "There's no way I can keep this up 'til home."

"Don't speak. Just run. You won't need to. We just need to get to the wall to the park."

They reached the verge on the other side of the carriageway then ran up the shallow embankment, into the tall grass, and finally past the shrubs and into the trees. Wren looked back again. All the creatures were still heading in their direction, but the cover of the woods would help lose some of them at least. "Try and weave, Bobbi. Let's see if we can use the cover of the trees to confuse them."

They ran for another few seconds, but then Robyn began to slow down. "I can't carry on. I can't carry on running."

Wren put a firm hand on her back. "We don't have a choice. Not much farther now, just keep going." Wren looked back again, the two sisters were weaving in and out of the trees as well as they could, nevertheless, Wren could still make out some of the creatures clumsily making their way through the woods. She pressed harder against her sister's back.

"I can't...go...any...faster," Robyn protested in between breaths. Wren looked back again and now, two or three of the moving figures seemed to have gained some ground.

"Shit!" Wren said. "Keep going. Keep going the way we came. I'll catch up."

"No. You can't leave me," Robyn protested as she began to slow down again.

Wren kept pushing her. "Don't you dare slow down. Run as fast as you can, Bobbi. I'll be back behind you in no time at all." Robyn sped up again, gave her sister one last fleeting look, and then Wren stopped.

She ran to her right. "*Aaaggghhh!!*" she screamed at the top of her voice, hitting the javelin against trees as she went. Suddenly, all the creatures who were within earshot or sight of Wren turned and headed towards her. She paused for a second to make sure still more shifted momentum in her direction. Wren looked back towards her sister, but she was already out of view of both her and the creatures, so half the battle was won. She put her head down and ran, holding the javelin in front of her, allowing it to cut a path through the woods. The growls increased in volume as she counted in her head. *Twenty-three, twenty-four, twenty-five* and go. She made a sharp right and began heading up the incline again in a diagonal. She looked back. The creatures were cutting across towards her. There were nowhere near as many as had stormed out of the trading estate, but as she glanced through the trees, she was confident there were still upwards of a dozen.

The nearest was just ten metres back, as the second change of direction had served in its favour. The one thing she had going for her was she was an experienced runner. It was in her blood; it was what she lived for it was—she went sprawling as her foot caught on a tree root. The javelin slid out of her hand and skidded across the woodland floor like a torpedo. Wren scrambled to her feet, not daring to look behind her but hearing the gurgling growls increase in volume.

She picked up the javelin and began to sprint, catching movement out of the corner of her eye and seeing more creatures beginning to converge on her as she almost doubled back. She angled left, heading further up the incline, off the clear-cut path, but in the direction she needed to go. Wren zigged and zagged, but now, after her earlier mistake, she kept a close eye on the ground in front of her, making sure there were no more obstacles to trip over. The volume of the creatures' howling did not dissipate, but it did not grow any louder and she threw a quick glance over her shoulder. She had managed to put a little more distance between herself and her nearest pursuers. She looked right; there were no more creatures coming towards her from that direction either, but she could not afford to let up the pace.

Her thighs began to strain as she continued to move upwards, but then she was back on a well-beaten path as she turned right once more. Ahead she could see the tramp creature she had speared when they had first entered the woods; she only hoped Robyn had already reached the wall because now everything was down to split second timing.

Wren continued to sprint. She reached the fallen creature then turned left up the embankment. Finally, the wall was in view, and there was her sister, struggling to make it up. It was almost an action replay of before. Her arms were over the top and she was desperately trying to swing her foot onto the ridge of the wall, but it just kept rising then falling like a broken clock hand swinging between twenty past and half past.

"Shit," hissed Wren as she scrabbled up the steep embankment, grasping the odd branch with her left hand to give her more purchase. She looked back to see the beasts all still in the full throes of pursuit but struggling with the gradient of the incline. Finally, she reached the top and hurled the javelin over the wall, grabbed her sister's feet and pushed them upwards as hard and fast as she could.

"*Aaaggghhh!*" her sister screamed as she launched over the wall like an acrobat leaving a cannon. Wren cast one final look back to see the outstretched hands of the creatures just a matter of feet away from her. She jumped up, grabbing the top of the wall and swinging her foot up. Her boot made firm contact with the wall's ridge for the briefest of seconds before she jumped down the other side.

She remained crouched, resting her back against the wall as the creatures began to batter themselves against it, hopelessly. Wren got her breathing back under control as she watched her sister pick herself up from the ground.

"Thanks. I guess," Robyn said, her breathing ragged.

Wren looked out over the park. It was still fairly early. "Come on. We'll rest when we get home," she said, picking up the javelin.

"Can we just have one minute?"

"The longer we're out here, the greater the risk," Wren replied.

"Fine. I'll take the risk. Just one minute," Robyn said, crouching down and taking several deep breaths to try and regulate her breathing. The thuds and growls continued, and it was not long before the two of them resumed their journey.

They remained silent, still in shock at the events that had unfolded. The two sisters carried on through the park, looking around them, making sure there were no more unwanted admirers, keeping a tight hold of their javelins. They finally reached the fence bordering McIntyre's field, and they clambered over. They remained silent as they walked through the long grass and it was not until they reached their family home that the true weight of what had happened hit them. Not only had they not made it out of the city, they had nearly been killed and they had lost two rucksacks full of supplies, clothes, their "prized possessions," and some weapons. They were in one piece for the time being, but the prognosis was not good. Their first full day as orphans in this new world had started badly. As they crawled through the hole in the bottom of the fence and into their back garden, the cold dew washed over their hands. As they realised they no longer had a mother and father to make everything better, both girls began to sob.

6

They had washed the dirt and the horrors of the morning off themselves in a sink of cold soapy water. All the curtains at the front of the house had been closed. They did not want to see what was going on out in the street, nor did they want whoever or whatever was on the street to see what was going on in their home

They had changed into fresh clothes and were both sat on the bed in Wren's room. "So, what now?" asked Robyn.

"I think we need to learn to fight before we head out there again," Wren said.

"What are you talking about? Head out there again, *are you mad?!* I mean, what's next? We've got no food. We don't know how long the water will carry on running. We've got no electricity. We'll be lucky if we last more than a couple of days in our own home, never mind out there in the world."

"So, what do you think we should do? Just sit here and hope?"

"I don't know, but there's no way I'm going back out there. I was right all along. We should have just stayed here, but nooo, Miss Heptathlete Medal Winning I Always Knows Better Bitch, had to have her own way."

"Look, we need to work together. There's stuff we need to do. For a start we—"

"Just shut up, Wren. Shut your big flapping gob. I'll tell you what I'm going to do. I'm going to go to my room. I'm going to put my head on my pillow and I'm going to sleep."

"You're not the only one who's hurting. We both lost our parents yesterday. You think I've forgotten? You think I don't care?"

"If you care, why are you just carrying on, making plans?"

"That's not fair. I'm just trying to keep us safe. It's what Mum and Dad would have wanted."

Robyn stood up and marched out, she went into her room and closed the door. Wren sat there on the bed for a while, then she lay down with her legs dangling off the edge. She stared at the ceiling, wracking her brains, desperate to come up with a solution to the problem. At this moment, the prospect of escaping the city looked further away than ever, but she knew that's what they needed to do if they were going to live. After a few moments of contemplation, she stood up and headed downstairs. She walked into the kitchen and began to rifle through all the cupboards. She knew there was a little food that they had not been able to fit in the rucksacks, but there was not a huge amount. She pulled it all out and lined it up on the counter. There were two tins of baked beans, a tin of sweetcorn, a tin of corned beef, a packet of dried spaghetti. There was a tube of tomato paste, a large jar of pickled onions left over from Christmas, and two packets of dried custard. "Shit," she said looking at the sorry array of foodstuffs in front of her.

She headed out of the kitchen, into the hall, and quietly unlocked the back door, stepping out into the garden. She looked towards the large hole in the back fence, then looked to her right at the hole in the neighbour's fence. If they were stopping here for a while, those would need to be blocked. Wren opened the rear door to the garage. She left it open, as the only torch she had was in a rucksack under a bush at a trading estate some distance away. The car was parked in the driveway; her dad had been loading it up when their world had come crashing in on them. She stepped into the darkness. The faintest crack of light appeared underneath the up and over door, which was securely locked. She hunted around the shelving units and picked up a small toolbox which she transported outside. She opened it up to see screwdrivers, spanners, pliers, spirit levels, and a wide array of nails and screws. She removed a couple of the screwdrivers and put them in her pocket before walking back into the garage and searching the remainder of it thoroughly for what she was looking for, but to no avail. She headed back into the house and through to the kitchen. She shot glances in every direction, looking for inspiration, until she went to the wall cupboards and began to examine the doors. She pulled one of the screwdrivers out and was about to start removing one of the doors when she looked across the breakfast bar to the huge Monet print on the wall in the dining room.

Wren removed it from the wall and examined the back. It had a hardboard backing. "Perfect," she said, beginning to dismantle the frame. She removed the wood and leant the remainder of the frame against the wall. She headed into the living room and did the same to another print in there, before heading back out to the garden.

Wren went back to the toolbox, and as much as she'd like to hammer nails into the fences for speed, screwing the boards into place would be a lot safer. She had seen her dad use some kind of metal spike to bore holes in wood for screws. She picked it up by its red plastic handle and pressed hard in the four corners of the first piece of wood. Before turning four screws in just by a couple of threads, not too deep, like she had seen her dad do. She took the first piece of board over to the back fence and put it in place. It was way too big for the gap, but that did not matter; at least it covered it. She began to turn the screw, forcing it through the solid hardboard and into the wooden post. She repeated the process with the next screw, then the other two went into much softer fence panels. It was not very secure. But it blocked the view, which was her primary concern.

Wren opened the shed and took out a spade which she dug into the soil and wedged against the piece of hardboard. She stood back, admiring her handy work for a moment before starting on the next repair.

She looked at her hands; small blisters had appeared on the palms, which she traced proudly. The repairs did not make the fences invulnerable, but that had not been the goal. It was merely to make anyone in the garden invisible to those in the garden to the right or the field to the back. Wren intended to spend time out here training, and if one of those things happened by, she wanted to minimise the chance of her being seen.

She put the tools back in the box, headed into the house, and straight into the kitchen. That work had made her thirsty. She pulled a mug from the tree and filled it. She drank greedily, and water ran over her chin and down her front. Wren refilled the mug and did the same again. Then she paused with her handle still on the tap. She filled her mug again and placed it carefully onto the counter, then did same with all the other mugs. She opened the kitchen cupboards and began to fill bowls, jugs, flasks, glasses, Tupperware containers, until all the surfaces in the kitchen were covered.

Wren pulled a bucket out from under the sink and turned the tap on then headed back out to the garage and grabbed the bucket that her dad used for washing the car. She filled that too. Then she went upstairs, placed the plug in the bath, and turned the tap on. At least if the water did go off, they would have a supply which would last them a while.

Wren headed back across the landing, passing her sister's closed door on the way. She went into her own room and opened her bedside cabinet drawer, pulling out a small project book and a pencil. She sat down on the bed and started writing a list. Water, tick. Fence repairs in back garden, tick. Food, question mark. She took the book and headed downstairs to look at the food that was still laid out on the counter.

"Okay, by no stretch of the imagination can you put a tick against this one," she said, placing the book down by the side of the food. She looked at her watch. It was eleven-thirty. She had been up for six and a half hours. If nothing else, she needed to finish this day with some hope, but looking at the meagre selection of foodstuffs in front of her made her realise that the only way that was going to happen was if she went back out there.

Wren tapped her pen against her mouth. *Where am I going to get more food with a minimal amount of risk?* Then she remembered back to the horrific scene from the previous day, when her neighbours next door but one had turned. She headed straight to the cupboard underneath the kitchen sink and pulled out a couple of reusable shopping bags, the kind that had shoulder straps. Wren folded and twisted them as tight as she could, binding them with a couple of thick rubber bands from the bureau drawer, and wedging them into her jacket pocket.

She headed out into the hall and looked up the stairs, passing on the idea of shouting up to tell Robyn what she was doing. She stepped into the back garden; for a second she considered taking along the javelin, but then thought for the distance and the enclosed spaces she was going to be confined to, a smaller weapon would be better. She went back to her dad's toolbox and picked out a claw hammer. She really wished she hadn't slid the crowbar into her rucksack; that would have been perfect.

Wren pulled a white plastic lawn chair across to the fence and climbed onto it, peeking over into the next garden. It was all clear. She had no idea if her next-door neighbours were safe and hiding or...she still could not bring herself to think about the alternative. She took two deep breaths and vaulted the six-foot barrier, landing softly on her neighbour's lawn. She remained there, frozen for a moment to see if a family of ghouls were going to run towards her. When none did, she jogged the few feet across to the other side and leapt over the hedge that acted as the divide between her next-door neighbours and Catriona and Brian's garden. She paused again, looking in all directions to make sure the coast was clear before carrying on.

Wren walked up to the large living room window and cupped her hands over her eyes to look in without the reflection of the sun dazzling her. She knew nobody lived with Brian and Catriona, and she felt sure they would not have returned to the house after...after it happened. Zombies were a lot of things, but didn't seem like the indoorsy types. She walked up to the back door and tried the handle. "Bingo," she whispered as she pushed the door open and stepped inside.

The interior was cool, and she breathed in deeply. There was no smell of decay. As she listened, there was no gurgling or growling, so she walked farther into the house. She looked up the staircase; it was clear. She looked down the hall. The living room door was open. She had already seen from outside that was clear. She put her hand on the door handle to the dining room/kitchen and clenched her fist tightly around the shaft of the hammer. She pushed the door open quickly and took a step back. The front door was closed. A few seconds passed by and nothing came towards her, so she stepped into the dining room and looked right to the open plan kitchen. It was all clear.

Part of her wanted to start going through the kitchen cupboards straight away, but that nagging little paranoid part of her told her she needed to check upstairs first. Even though the likelihood of anything being up there was astronomically small, she knew she had to be sure. Wren stepped back out into the hall and stood for a moment at the bottom of the steps, looking up. Should she walk up slowly and stealthily? Or should she charge up, flying into the face of anything that came out, head on?

"Screw it!" She ran up the stairs, two at a time, vaulting onto the landing and ending the fluid sequence in a frozen crouch. Wren paused. Five, six, seven…but nothing came. She stood up and began to go room to room, swinging the doors open, popping her head around the corner and straight on to the next, all the time clutching the shaft of the hammer like her life depended on it, which of course, it did. Satisfied there was nobody else in the house, she went back through the rooms, closing all the curtains. She did the same downstairs. If any of those creatures were out in the street, she did not want to attract their attention.

Wren headed back to the kitchen, placed the two bags on the kitchen surface, and got to work rifling through the cupboards.

*

Tears streaked Robyn's cheeks as she lay in bed. The buds remained in her ears despite the last of the battery dying on her phone. She had been listening to *The Show Must Go On* by Queen. It was her dad's favourite band and that was his favourite track. Most of what he listened to was lame, but Robyn liked quite a few Queen songs and she had downloaded her favourites. Now they would fade into distant memory. As the battery died, she wondered if she'd ever hear another Queen song.

She stared at the ceiling and wondered, *how long have I been lying here?* She remembered drifting off to sleep at one stage, the trauma of the morning being too much for her. Robyn stayed there for a few more minutes before sitting up and placing the phone on her bedside cabinet. Now it was nothing more than an ornament. She opened the bedroom door and walked into Wren's room. Seeing her sister was not there, she went downstairs into the kitchen. "What the hell?" she asked as she saw all the bowls, mugs, bottles and jugs filled with water. All the food was collected together in one neat pile as well, and her confusion grew. "Wren?" she called.

When Robyn got no reply, she headed into the living room. There was no sign of her in there either. She started to get an uneasy feeling, the kind a dog gets when it's delivered to the boarding kennels with its favourite toy, and it just stands there watching its owners climb back into the car and drive away. She ran through the house and into the garden. Makeshift repairs had been done to the fences, but there was no sign of her sister. She went into the garage. "*Wren?*" she whispered, but there was no sign. "She's left me. She's gone without me."

Robyn sat on the white garden chair. The sun beat down as it rose higher and higher into the sky. On any day when the world had not just fallen into the depths of hell, life would have been good. But today, the bright sun and the warm breeze went unappreciated. "I can't believe she's left me."

7

A look of pure elation adorned Wren's face as she loaded the second bag with tins and packets of food. She had not finished by a long way, but there were enough supplies in these cupboards to keep them going for a few weeks, at least. She would not be able to get it all back in one journey. In fact, she would probably have to make several trips, but food was most definitely ticked off the list now. She lifted the bag off the surface and realised there was no way she would be able to get over the fence carrying it, so she removed a few of the tins until the weight was not so prohibitive. She placed the carry strap over her head and shoulder, picked up the hammer and went through the house to the back door. She opened it slowly and peeked out. All clear. Wren climbed over the first fence and kept her eyes glued to the windows of her neighbour's house as she walked through the garden to her own fence. She took the bag from her shoulder and pushed the bulk of it over, keeping a tight hold of the straps. She lowered it until she could reach no further, then let it drop as carefully as she could. It made a crunching sound as it landed in one of her mum's soft flower beds.

Wren took hold of the top of the fence and pulled herself up. She let out a small gasp of surprise as she saw Robyn standing there, holding a javelin in her shaking hands.

"Wren!" Robyn cried, dropping the javelin and running towards her sister as the young athlete landed next to the dropped bag. Robyn threw her arms around Wren and squeezed her. "I thought you'd left me."

"What? Why would you think that?"

"I woke up and there was no sign of you, and you'd filled all those bowls and things with water. And put all the food out."

Wren picked up the bag and the two of them went into the house. "I wouldn't leave you. What kind of person do you think I am?"

"I thought maybe you realised you were better off by yourself."

"No...course not. But we need to work together, Bobbi, starting now. I've found a load of food next door but one. It will keep us going for weeks. It'll take me half the time to get it here if you give me a hand."

Robyn looked at the bag. "I don't understand."

"You don't understand what?" Wren asked, as she opened the door and carried the bag to the kitchen.

Robyn followed her. "I don't understand. This morning you were all for us getting out of here, now you're talking about having enough food to last us weeks."

Wren placed the bag on a stool and began to pile up the food next to their own meagre supply. Robyn watched as packets of biscuits and instant mashed potato, tins of beans and spaghetti, jars of hot dogs and all sorts of other foods that made her mouth begin to water came out of the bag.

"We can't stay here forever, but after this morning I realised heading out the way we were was going to get us killed sooner rather than later. As far as fighting goes, I don't have any technique at the moment. I'm going to train myself how to fight, the way I train myself how to do anything."

"You are such a nerd."

"Yeah, well, you're going to train too."

"Dream on."

"We're going to have to learn how to fight, or we're not going survive."

"I'm a lover, not a fighter," Robyn said, beginning to get back to her usual snarky self.

"Okay. You can love these things to death the next time one of them tries to attack you. I'm going to learn how to defend myself so when we head out again, we're in better shape."

"Right now, I'm not even thinking about heading back out there."

"Whatever. First things first. We'll get the rest of this food. Will you at least help me do that?"

"I suppose."

Wren gave Robyn a look bordering on disdain before rolling her eyes and heading back out with the empty shopping bag. Her sister followed her. Wren put the white garden chair next to the fence again, and now, conscious of the fact that Robyn was coming with her, got hold of another, and lifted it over the fence, lowering it down onto the other side.

"We need to stay quiet. We don't know who or what could be around."

"Well, duh!"

Wren gave Robyn another look before heading over the fence once more. Robyn followed her, struggling less with the tall fence now there were steps on either side. Within less than a minute, the pair of them were back in their neighbour's kitchen, loading more food into the bags. "Don't overfill them," Wren said, "We don't want them too heavy to lift over the fence."

"Water's wet. Snow is cold. Fire is hot," Robyn replied.

"What are you talking about?"

"Oh, I thought we were stating the obvious to each other for no reason."

"Why do you have to be such an utter bitch?"

"Where do you get off always thinking you can tell me what to do?"

The two of them fell silent, filling the bags and ferrying them back home. On the final journey to the neighbour's house, Wren took out all the bowls and jugs as she had at her own house.

"We can't carry all those back home, we'll spill it all trying to get over the fence."

"Duh!" Wren said this time. "We'll have a supply of water here just in case anything happens."

Robyn did not respond, she did not want to know what her sister meant by *anything*, but a look of understanding swept over her face. She glanced at the clock on the wall. It was nearly one p.m. "I'm famished," she said.

"I just want to have a look around to see if they've got anything else we can use, then we'll have some lunch."

"Anything else to use? Like what?"

"I don't know. Maybe they've got a camp stove or something. Can't do any harm to look."

The two girls went through the house room to room, checking every drawer and cupboard. Robyn took a couple of Catriona's tops that she liked the look of, as well as a nail painting kit. "Seriously?" Wren asked.

"It's not like there's going to be anything good to watch on TV."

Wren shook her head. "How about picking up a book and learning something?"

"Don't worry, I already know how to be a boring nerd who has no friends. So come on, show me what you got."

Wren had put everything she had found into a pillowcase. She'd found plasters, antiseptic ointment, painkillers, bandages, a sewing kit, batteries, two small torches and candles. "Oh, and I found this too," she said, breaking out into a wide smile and pulling an odd-looking contraption with wires and connectors from the case.

"What the hell is that?"

"It's a solar charger for our phones."

"Oh my god! Tell me it's got the connector we need for ours. Tell me, please!"

"It's got connectors for most phones by the look of it, but yes, it's got the one for ours."

"Oh my god!" Robyn said again. She took the solar charger and examined it more closely.

"C'mon. Let's get all this stuff back and we'll get something to eat."

Robyn was suddenly a lot more buoyant as they made the final journey back home. They got into the house and she immediately ran up the stairs with the solar charger and hooked it up to her mobile phone, taking it and the charger out onto the landing and placing it in the window overlooking the back garden. "Wren!" she called.

"What?" Wren asked walking to the bottom of the stairs.

"Come see if I've done it right."

Wren had a jar of olives in one hand and a tin of rice pudding in the other, but this was the happiest she'd seen her sister in the last two days and maybe, just maybe, if she could maintain her levity for a while, her sister might stop being such a bitch.

Wren placed the jar and the can down and adjusted the small solar panels and checked the connector was firmly in the phone. "Yep, all set up. It won't be as quick as a plugin, but at least it will charge."

Robyn smiled. "Thanks," she said, and the two of them headed down the stairs to have lunch.

*

After lunch, Robyn went back upstairs while Wren began to put all the food away in the cupboards. There was very little surface space with all the water bottles and bowls, and although that had not been an issue when she had gathered together the small amount of food from their own cupboards, now they had a proper supply, it was.

It reminded her of when they had gone to get the Christmas shopping that time they were having twelve people for Boxing Day dinner. Dad had brought in a never-ending succession of carrier bags from the car. Wren finished putting the last bits and pieces away before reaching across for her project book. She proudly ticked the food entry. Another mission accomplished.

She stood there with her hands on her hips, looking around the kitchen. Things were a little brighter now. They had food, and they had water for the time being; it had been a good day's work. There had been no screams or shouts from outside like there had the previous day. They lived on a quiet, long, cul-de-sac, and there was no logical reason an army of savage creatures would descend upon them unless they were in pursuit of someone. It was not perfect by any stretch of the imagination, but maybe they could last out here, long enough for Wren to figure out what she needed to figure out.

She headed to the back garden again and picked up one of the javelins leaning against the outside wall. The internet had gone down some time before the power clicked off the previous day. What she would not give now for a Teach Yourself Bojutsu! video, or better still, a book about it. As she stood there in the afternoon sun, she realised how futile it was to think that she could learn something it took people years to master, but then she remembered the advice she had given to her sister the previous day. *Outline your objectives.* There was just one simple objective, and that was not to die. Really, the only two surefire ways of achieving that were A: avoid the reanimated creatures completely, or B: kill them...again. Wren looked down at the javelin in her hand. Throwing it was the easiest thing in the world for her; it was one of her best events in the heptathlon, but using it as a spear, or fighting pole, was going to require a different mindset.

She stood with her legs apart and got used to the feel of the long metal spear in both hands. She passed it from left to right, over and over, then swept it through the air. It made a whooshing sound like the hockey stick had earlier that day. She took it back in both hands and thrust it forward and up, imagining she was driving it through the head of one of the creatures. Earlier that day, her hands had been shaking as she came face to face with one. *That was only natural*, she told herself. It was the first time, and with everything that had happened, it was madness to think she could just pick up a weapon and become a zombie slayer.

She strode forward and thrust again, then again, then again. She spun around, imagining she was in some *Crouching Tiger, Hidden Dragon* sequel, and thrust again, strode forward, then thrust again. The javelin was very light in her hands, and the more she held it, the more she used it, the more it just felt like an extension of herself. This time when it came to turning, she swept the javelin round slicing the air and making that satisfying sound once again. She carried out this regimental exercise more than a dozen times before pausing. She looked towards the washing line. It was all well and good having imaginary foes to battle in her head, but if she was going to achieve accuracy in a real-life situation, she was going to need targets to fine-tune her skills.

*

Robyn was looking forward to her phone charging so she could zone out again with some of her favourite music. She was not going to listen to Queen for a while.

She realised their songs would act as a trigger and just make her emotional. She wanted to grieve, but Wren's attitude was freaking her out. The whole: *we need to get organised, we need supplies, we need to train* thing just made her feel hollow, sad, a little sick, and a little angry. Their parents had died. The world was coming to an end; it was right to grieve. It was natural. But Wren had gone into some kind of mad overdrive. She had always been weird, but now she was acting much weirder than usual.

Robyn looked out the window. Two doors down on the other side of the road, she noticed that the curtains were all closed, just like in their own house. Surely that meant there were people alive in there, too. More to the point, she knew the eldest son was a year older than her and really hot. If it came to repopulating the planet, Robyn was more than happy to give it a go with him. *It would be for mankind and stuff.* She allowed herself a small smile.

Just then, she saw the curtains in one of the bedrooms twitch a little before being pulled to one side. From what she could make out, it was one of the younger brothers. The curtain closed again as quickly as it had opened and everything went still. Robyn moved her head closer to the window and looked farther down the street. There were a couple more houses with closed curtains. This was good. She could not see past the bend, but it was a sign of life. The road they lived on was made up entirely of old, brick-built semi-detached dwellings. Some had garages attached, some did not. Some had enclosed front gardens, some had open driveways, but all of them had back gardens that were inaccessible without going through the house or opening a tall wooden side gate. None of the back gardens were visible from the road, and certainly not on her side of the street; the rear of the surrounding houses looked out over McIntyre's field. There were plenty more dangerous places to be.

Robyn went out onto the landing and looked at the solar charger. *God, how long is this thing going to take?*

Then she caught movement out of the corner of her eye and saw Wren in the back garden, dancing around with a javelin.

"Seriously? What a dork."

She went downstairs and headed out into the back garden as Wren thrust her javelin into a pair of her father's overalls she had put up on the line.

Robyn continued to watch her for a moment. "It's the head you have to aim for. What good is that going to do?"

"I'm all out of heads," Wren said, "I'm just building up my accuracy right now."

"Oh yeah? How's that working out for you?" Robyn asked with a snarky grin on her face.

"Pretty good," replied Wren, not rising to the bait.

"The Donovans have got their curtains closed. I saw one of the younger brothers looking out earlier."

"Oh."

"Do you think we should go across?"

"Why?"

"Well, y'know, other survivors. We might be able to help each other."

"We don't need help. We've got food, we've got water, we've got weapons. The Donovans don't strike me as thinking types; where would the benefit be to us?"

"The benefit would be that if something happened, we'd have people who could help us."

"Look. If you want to go over there. Go over there. I don't want them here. I don't want anything to do with them. I don't like the Donovans, especially Carl. He's an idiot, and he's not a nice person. None of them are nice people."

Robyn stood there pouting. "There are other houses with closed curtains, too."

"Great," Wren replied, as she thrust and swiped at the mid-section of the overalls.

"Don't you want to make contact with some of them at least?"

"Why?"

"God you're impossible," Robyn said, storming off. "I hate you sometimes."

Wren gave her a sideways glance as she unleashed another flurry of stabs on the boiler suit.

8

Wren had been training in the garden for two hours. She headed back into the house and went upstairs to the bathroom. She turned on the cold water tap which coughed and spluttered, releasing a few spits of water, and then nothing.

"Dammit," Wren said. She turned the hot water tap onto a trickle. She knew they would have a full tank until it ran dry. She stripped down, released a few inches of water, and had the best wash she could in the sink before changing into some fresh clothes. She neatly folded her tracksuit; it was not going to smell great after a few more training sessions, but laundry was not really going to be an option.

Robyn's door was closed, and Wren hovered outside for a moment before going in. Her sister was stood at the window, looking down the street. "The water's gone off," Wren said.

"Shit! Already?"

"Yeah. You'd think it was the end of the world or something."

"At least we've got a good supply."

"For the time being. It won't last forever."

"This is Scotland. It never stops raining."

"True. Are you going to go over?"

"I haven't decided yet," she said, looking down towards the van that had gone through their neighbour's front room.

"Every time we go out, it will be a risk."

"Duh! I figured that out this morning."

"If you think it's worth the risk heading over there, then you go over. But you put both of us in danger by doing it."

"How's that?"

"Do you think those boneheads will have thought about getting supplies together, or the water going off? Do you think they'll have planned beyond closing the curtains and keeping the fridge cool as long as they can so their beer doesn't get warm?"

Robyn fell silent, for the first time acknowledging that her desire to see Carl Donovan was based on nothing more than physical attraction. "So if the water's gone off, I'm guessing we're going to have to fill the cistern from the bath."

Wren laughed. "Yeah, good one."

"What do you mean?"

"We've got like one flush in the upstairs and downstairs toilet, and then that's it. We're going to have to use a bucket and tip it outside."

"Gross. No way! You can do that. I'm not taking a piss or a dump in a bucket and tipping it outside. Eugh!"

"You need to start thinking, Robyn. What would you rather have? Water to drink or water to flush the toilet?"

"We've got loads of water. We've got a bath full. We've got all the stuff downstairs. We've got all the stuff at Catriona's place, not to mention when it rains again."

"And how are we going to gather the rainwater? Do you honestly believe having creature comforts is more important than drinking water?"

"Creature comforts! You make it sound like using the toilet is a luxury."

"Today, it is a luxury. Yesterday it wasn't, maybe, but today it is."

Tears appeared in Robyn's eyes. "I can't take much more of this."

"What? Reality?"

"Just get out of my room. I want to be alone."

"Gladly," Wren replied, marching out and closing the door behind her. She went straight into her bedroom and flopped onto the bed. Her eyes were immediately drawn to the holdall on top of her wardrobe. If something happened and they had to get out of the house quickly, they would not last long without supplies. As fast as she flopped down onto the bed, she sprang up again and reached up for her holdall. She took it downstairs and into the kitchen, where she started to fill it with food, medical supplies, a couple of good knives and screwdrivers, water and a few odds and ends. She took the holdall into the garden and placed it inside the shed, right by the door, just in case.

She started heading back into the house, then looked at the javelin leaning up against the outside wall. She picked it up, and after just one training session, felt much more comfortable with it. She spun it around her head before bringing it down on top of some imaginary foe. She swished and swooshed and thrust and batted, making short work of the half dozen creatures that were running towards her in her mind's eye.

A small smile crept across her face. She closed her eyes and took a deep breath; she was taking charge of things again.

Wren was ripped from her peaceful moment by the sound of a loud engine, followed by a second, and then an almost deafening crunch of metal against cement.

It was the street. Something was happening out on the street. She ran into the house, dropping the javelin in the doorway before leaping up the stairs. She burst into Robyn's room; her sister was glued to the window.

"What was that?" Wren asked.

"They're blockading the end of the street," she replied with an excited look on her face.

"Who is?"

"The Donovans, The Barkers, and another family from further down the street. They've pulled four transits across the entrance. Wall to wall. They've backed them into one another too, so there's no gap. The rest of them are throwing wheelie bins and all sorts on to build a barrier."

Wren squeezed in next to Robyn to look up the street. Two creatures appeared and charged forward, battering their bodies against the side of the engine compartment of the middle van. At the same time, a garden bench crunched down on the metal bonnet, hiding the attacking dead from Wren and Robyn's view. They saw the heads of more beasts, but those were hidden as quickly as the first by a hail of debris, sacks of garden rubbish, an old wardrobe. The barrier was constructed in no time at all, leaving the creatures invisible on the other side.

"See! I told you. Now what are we going to look like to them for not helping?"

Wren gave her sister a long look. "What is it you think they've done?"

"They've blockaded the street. They've made us safe."

"They've made a load of noise. Now every creature out there knows there's a buffet waiting on our street. We'll be under constant attack."

"But the barrier. They can't get through. Look at it," Robyn said, pointing. "It's getting higher and wider by the second."

The two of them watched as Carl Donovan and one of his brothers carried more black sacks out of one of the houses and threw them onto the barricade.

"I still say we were safer when nothing knew we were here, and we had more than one escape route."

"Yeah, well, I think it's a great idea."

"I'm sure you do."

"Y'know what. Screw this," Robyn said, turning and heading out. Wren heard her feet pound down the stairs and the front door slam, before watching her sister run towards the barrier and the throng of activity. Robyn went straight up to Carl Donovan and the two of them disappeared into a house, reappearing a moment later carrying a pine TV cabinet. After a few minutes of frantic to-ing and fro-ing, carrying and heaving, everything began to calm down. Wren continued watching, and her heart sank when she saw Robyn pointing in the direction of the house.

She kept a vigil at the window, and to her relief, as the crowd began to dissipate, Robyn headed back towards the house alone. Wren went downstairs and met her as she entered. "Why did you point towards the house?"

"What?"

"Why did you point over here when you were talking earlier?"

"I was just saying you were back here. You had hurt your back, otherwise, you'd have come to help. Don't worry! I'm not going to give away any big secrets like you're mistrustful, paranoid and you think you're better than everybody else. As if that's much of a secret. They've been working on checking the whole street. After yesterday, they kept eyes on the *turned*, and where they went. They've got walkie-talkies to stay in touch with each other. When they'd figured out the street was clear, they rallied together and came up with a plan to blockade it." Wren remained silent. "You don't like the fact that you were wrong and I was right. I told you we should have made contact instead of hiding away here by ourselves."

"I still say it was a mistake, but what's done is done."

"Whatever."

"I was thinking we should probably have cereal for tea before the milk goes off."

"Ooh, sounds awesome, but we've been invited to go over and eat across at the Donovans. They're having the other families around to have a big barbecue."

"You aren't serious."

"Donnie and Jan said it was sensible to use up all the meat now the fridges and freezers had all stopped working. They said it would be a good way for everybody to get to know each other too."

"Who are Donnie and Jan? And why are you even entertaining such a stupid idea?"

"Donnie and Jan are Carl's mum and dad, and it's not a stupid idea. It's very sensible. It's feeding people while avoiding waste, and it would make sense to get to know everyone. There is going to be a guard posted at the barricade twenty-four-seven, so you don't need to freak about that either. They invited you too, by the way."

"I'll pass."

"There's a surprise. You'd only spoil it if you went. There'll be booze there and little Miss Goody-Two-Shoes can't take her drink, so everybody but you would be enjoying themselves. Probably just as well you stay here. You'd only bring everyone down. And I could do with getting hammered. Our parents died yesterday, and to you, it's like it never happened. Getting pished would help me forget that for just a little while. It would help me forget that my world has collapsed and I'm stuck with you." Robyn pulled off her T-shirt and walked out of the kitchen. "I'm going to get changed," she shouted behind her as she ran up the stairs.

Wren slumped into a chair. Why was her sister so cruel? She was grieving, but everyone grieved in different ways, at different speeds. Staying busy helped Wren occupy her mind while she actually came to grips with what had happened.

Wren remained seated as her sister re-entered the kitchen diner. She had changed into a new pair of jeans and a new top, she had applied make-up and looked more like she was going for a night out on the town than someone who was living through the apocalypse.

"Don't wait up," Robyn said as she headed out and slammed the door behind her.

Wren continued to sit there as tears began to roll down her face. She had suffered insults and barbs all through growing up—not just from Robyn, but from kids at school too. When they had been too much for her to handle, her mum and dad had always made things better. But now, for the first time in her life, she realised just how alone she was, and it hurt. After a few more minutes, she dabbed the tears from her face with the bottom of her t-shirt and stood up. This would do her no good. Let the idiots have their end of the world barbecue party. Wren had eaten plenty of meals alone.

She poured herself a big bowl of the sweetest, unhealthiest cereal she could see. She drowned it in milk, which, although not cold, was still cooler than room temperature, and she began to shovel it into her mouth.

*

Robyn began to regret leaving Wren by herself soon after joining the rest of them at the party. More people had appeared as the two younger Donovan brothers had gone door to door announcing the barbecue. In total there were around thirty people in the enclosed back garden of the Donovan's. They had the same, six-foot panelled fencing that her dad had installed, and as she stood in Carl's bedroom looking out of the window, she could see it backed onto a small piece of waste ground before the dual carriageway. It seemed as safe as anywhere.

"So, what do you think?" Carl asked, nodding to the glass in her hand.

"Strong," she said, taking another sip.

"Yeah. Dad makes it himself. Gets the job done."

"Totally."

"Don't worry," he said, "We're safe. There's no danger anything is going to get past that barricade, and even if they did, there are a lot of us to fight. Anyway, those things aren't so tough."

"Really? You've dealt with one?"

"You could say that," Carl said.

"What happened?"

"It was yesterday afternoon. That's when Dad had the idea about the walkie-talkies. After the crash, when those things finally cleared off, I took one of the radios down to the Barker's."

"Where'd you get the radios from?"

"What?"

"Where did you get the radios?"

"They're my kid brother's, but that's beside the point. I dropped one off and on my way back, there was one just stood there in the middle of the road, just watching me."

"So, they're toy radios?"

Carl looked irritated. "They're not toys. They work. Anyway, I'm telling you. This thing was just looking at me. "And I was just stood there looking at it. Dad gave me a crowbar to take with me and I stood there with it in my hand, getting an idea for its weight, just getting a feel for it, cos I knew this thing was about to come for me." He took another long drink from his bottle. "Anyway, then it started towards me, putting its arms out and moaning. Before I knew what was happening, it was nearly on top of me, but I booted it away and it went flying. So, before it got up, I ran across and just smacked it over and over with the crowbar until it stopped moving. By the time I was done, there was blood everywhere. Blood on my hands, blood all over my face, everywhere," he said, smiling.

"Wow. You're really brave."

"Nothing to it. Like I say. They're not that scary if you know how to look after yourself. If anything happens, you just stick by me," he said, winking.

"Erm, I think they're dishing up down there," she said.

"Sweet. We'll get a bit to eat and then we can come back up here, play a bit of music and have a bit of a laugh."

"Erm, okay, yeah, that sounds… awesome."

9

Wren was lying in bed awake when she heard the front door bang closed. She hit the light button on her watch to see it was only ten-thirty. More clattering came from below, and she picked up the kitchen knife and torch that were sitting on her bedside table. Wren stood at her bedroom door for a few seconds then ran out of the door and down the stairs as fast as she could. She arrived in the kitchen, putting the torch on full beam, and saw Robyn face down on the floor.

"What the—" she put the knife down and helped her to her feet. "Are you drunk?"

"No, I'm not drunk! It's pitch black in here and I forgot a torch. I walked into one of the kitchen chairs and went flying.

"Ouch. Are you okay?"

"No," she said, pulling the chair upright and sitting down. "No, I'm not."

Wren put the torch down on the kitchen table and angled it away so there was enough light for them to see each other, without blinding them. "What's wrong?"

"You were right and I was wrong."

"About what?"

"I was wrong to leave you here by yourself for a start. And I was wrong to think those idiots know what they're doing."

"They've done a decent job with the blockade. I was watching it until it went dark. You can't see anything on the other side, so nothing on the other side can see us. They can't climb over it, so we're safe at the moment," Wren reassured her.

"Yeah, but if something does happen…that's when it will all go to shit. Carl told me he killed one of those things."

"Oh?"

"He was lying through his teeth. You and I have been up close with them. What he described was nothing like what we'd seen. It was like something a kid would come out with."

"So why did he say it?"

"Jesus, Wren, you really are naive. He was trying to get in my pants."

"I thought you liked him?"

"Yeah, well that lasted for about two minutes after I started talking to him. I don't mind them dumb, I don't mind them being cocksure of themselves, but I can't abide liars. Listen, I think you were right. I think this was a bad idea. The blockade."

"You're starting to worry me, Bobbi. What's changed? Did something happen over there?"

"Look, they're just…. It was like…"

"Tell me. What happened?"

"Carl's dad started talking about how he would sort out a roster for guarding the barricade and how he and John Barker would go house to house and make an inventory of everybody's supplies so they could be distributed fairly. It's like he's declared himself King of the Street. I can see things turning bad."

"Turning bad? So, everything's peachy right now?"

"You know what I mean. There's something else too. The Forth Road Bridge is a no go. There were pile-ups and the whole area is teeming with those things."

"How do you know?"

"The Barkers were there; they were going to head north."

"We'll figure it out. Look, let's get to bed, and get a good night's sleep we'll talk about this in the morning."

"Okay," Robyn replied, standing up. She gave Wren a hug. "Thanks for not saying, I told you so."

"Not my style. I'm more the silent gloating type."

Robyn laughed. "Bitch."

"Cow."

"Night night."

"Night, Bobbi."

*

Just after five-thirty a.m. the next morning, Wren stepped into the back garden with her javelin. She began by doing a number of bending and stretching exercises and was just about to begin practising her technique once again when she paused. A sound drifted into the air. It was not the usual sound of birds singing at this time of morning; in fact, the birds were noticeable by their absence. It was a steady chorus of low growls. Not just from two or three creatures, either. It was a full choir.

She heard the door open behind her and she swung round sharply. "It's just me," Robyn said, putting her hands up.

Half a smile crept onto Wren's face before her attention drifted back to the growls. "Can you hear them?"

Robyn lifted her head to listen. "Is that at the barricade?"

"I'm pretty sure."

"Shit!"

"Yeah!"

"I mean. There's no danger of them getting in or anything...is there?"

"I hope not."

"Me too."

"What are you doing up, anyway?"

"I thought about what you said. I thought about a lot. I want to train with you."

"You?"

"Yeah."

"Want to train?"

"Yeah."

"With me?"

"Yeah."

"Seriously?"

"Oh god! If you're going to be such a snarky bitch about it, forget it," Robyn said, turning around to head back inside.

"No...no. Don't go. I'm just...surprised. After yesterday I didn't think you wanted anything to do with this," she said, gesturing towards the overalls hanging on the washing line for target practice.

"After last night I realised there weren't going to be any knights in shining armour. I realised that nobody was coming to rescue us, and I realised that I couldn't leave everything to my kid sister. I'd have to take responsibility too."

"Erm, wow!"

"Wow, what?"

"I just didn't expect that."

"Look. Can I train with you? Or are you going to make a big thing out of this?"

"I'd love us to train together."

"Okay, so how do we do this?"

"We start by loosening up. We need to do some stretches and slowly ease into it, otherwise we might end up pulling something and then we're screwed."

"Okay, I'll follow you," Robyn said.

"Cool."

Wren performed a variety of warm-up exercises and Robyn followed her every move. When their bodies were sufficiently limber, they picked up their javelins, and Wren took Robyn through the thrust and advance sequence she had done the previous day. When her sister's moves looked confident, she had them performing the same moves single handed, right first, left second. They spent time targeting the overalls. Top left pocket. Right knee. Top right pocket. Left hip. They would never use any of these moves on one of the reanimated, but it was all about control and aim. That was the whole purpose behind the training. Everything was about becoming familiar with the weapon; familiar with the feel and the weight of it.

At just after eight a.m. they broke for breakfast. "Thanks, Wren," Robyn said, as they walked back into the house.

"That's okay. I'm happy to help."

"I feel better after that."

"We'll have another go later. It's true what they say, practice makes perfect."

"Cereal for breakfast?" Robyn asked, opening one of the cupboards.

"Yeah, sure," Wren replied.

"Hey, where's all the stuff gone? We had loads more than this"

"I took a few bits back to Brian's place; I took a few more and stashed them."

"How come?"

"If what you said last night is true, then we'll be getting a visit, and if they think we've got loads of supplies, it will cause us all sorts of problems. It's attention we can do without," Wren said.

"You think of everything, don't you?"

"There's another thing, Bobbi."

"What?"

"If things do go bad here. For whatever reason, I've put a bug-out bag underneath the tarpaulin in the shed. We grab it, we hop over the back fence, and we go back to plan A."

"What the hell's a bug-out bag?"

"It's like an emergency kit with enough stuff in to last us about seventy-two hours. It's got food, medical supplies, equipment and so on."

"That doesn't really fill me with confidence."

"Hey, it's just in case. It's better to have one and not need it than not have one and need it."

"I suppose you're right."

They'd just sat down at the table with their cereal when a knock came at the door. They shot glances towards each other. It was Robyn who got up to answer. She opened it to see Donnie, Carl, and Jason Barker, Donnie's right-hand man.

"Morning sunshine," Donnie said as he stepped in without invitation. "Morning, Wren, your back feeling better?"

Wren glared at him for a moment while she chewed on a mouthful of cereal. She swallowed it as she watched the other two men walk in behind him. "A bit," she said.

"Robyn probably told you, we're going to set up a communal pantry to make sure nobody goes hungry. So, we're going house to house, checking that people have got enough to last them for a few days, and taking any excess for a food bank." He looked over the kitchen counter. "I see you're pretty well sorted for water for a while anyway," he said, with a smile. "You don't mind if we look around, do you?"

The three men did not wait for an invitation and began opening cupboards straight away. "Erm, we don't have much," Robyn said as she stepped out of the way to let them by.

"We'll see, shall we? A couple of young girls like yourselves won't need much compared to some of the families on the street. We've got to make sure everybody is looked after."

Carl winked at Robyn as he passed by her, but she just looked away, feeling violated by the intrusion. The men went through the cupboards inspecting everything. Donnie Donovan pulled out a bag from his jacket pocket and started piling tins into it. "There's a lot here for two young girls," he said, filling the bag in no time, and getting out another.

"That's our stuff," Wren said, standing up from the table.

"There's no yours and mine anymore. We're all in this together now. We're setting up a food store at our house, and things are going to be rationed. You've got enough here to get you to the end of the week. Come to ours on Monday and we'll dish out enough for another week."

"If food's in such short supply, why did you waste it on a barbecue last night? All of a sudden we've got a food shortage, but you can waste pounds of meat having a party. How does that work?"

Donnie was about to answer when Carl stepped out of the kitchen area, past Robyn and walked straight up to Wren. Firstly, my dad doesn't need to answer to you. It was him who had the idea to blockade the street yesterday. He's a hero. You should be thanking him. Second, we were blowin' off a little steam after yesterday. That was hard work, not that you'd know, cos you were nowhere to be seen. And third, the meat was going to go off. I don't know if you've noticed, but all the fridges and freezers have stopped working around here."

"It's alright, son," Donnie said, putting his hand on Carl's shoulder. "Wren just needs to get used to how things are now."

Wren did not break her stare with Carl as he stood not a foot away from her, glaring down angrily. "Why didn't you cure the meat?"

"Cure it? There was nothing wrong with it. Why would it need curing?"

Wren raised an eyebrow and a small smirk curled up the corner of her face.

"What do you know about curing meat?" Donnie asked, gently pushing his son to one side.

"Only what I've read."

"So, you're a reader? We've got a smart one here, Jay," he said calling back to his pal who was closing the last of the kitchen cupboard doors. Donnie opened the bag and gave Wren a tin of rice pudding. There you go, girly. A bit of extra brain food for you. You keep reading your books, Wren. Always useful to have an educated person around," he said with a sarcastic smile. "We're coming up with a rota for guarding the barricade, and everybody will be taking a turn. We'll let you know soon enough when it's your shift. C'mon lads," he said, heading back out. Jason followed him, but before Carl left, he turned to look at Robyn.

"If you fancy coming round tonight, we're having leftovers from the barbie," he said.

"I'll check my calendar."

"Suit yourself," Carl replied. "I'll save you a nice piece of rump just in case." With that, he left, closing the door behind him.

The girls stood looking at each other for a moment, then burst out laughing. "*I'll save you a nice piece of rump?*" Wren said, bending over and holding her stomach. "Oh my god! What a complete prick. How could you have liked someone like that?"

"He was okay until he opened his big mouth." They continued laughing for a short time before Robyn went to look in the kitchen cupboards. "Shit, they've really ripped us off."

"We knew this was coming. I didn't leave anything in the cupboards I wasn't prepared to lose. We've still got enough to last us a few weeks; don't worry."

"We can't live on dry cereal. How are we going to cook stuff?"

"I was thinking about that." Wren walked into the kitchen and opened the oven door, pulling out one of the shelves. "Come with me," she said, and the two of them walked into the garden. Wren went behind the shed and pulled out the galvanised steel incinerator which her dad used for burning garden rubbish. She took off the lid and placed the oven shelf over the top of it. "Hey presto…we've got a hob again."

"Will that work?"

"Course it'll work. I'll make us something on it tonight...unless you want to go the barbie."

"Erm...no."

"Y'know things are going to get bad here. I mean *very bad*."

"How do you mean?"

"It's been one day and already they've resorted to a feudal rule. We've just been robbed and we're meant to be grateful that they're looking out for us. What comes next?"

"What does come next?"

"They're already doing whatever they want. They're going to continue that and take bigger and bigger liberties. What if they decide they prefer this house to their own? Or what if Carl decides he doesn't need to ask you for anything, and just takes it?" Her words hung in the air, and for the first time, Robyn grasped the true severity of what was going on.

"So what do we do?"

"We go back to the original plan."

"Grandad's place?"

"Yeah."

"I'm scared though, Wren. What happened yesterday, it showed me just how much I'm not cut out for this stuff."

"You think anybody's cut out for this? Look at the positives. We went out there, and we got back here in one piece. Next time, we'll know what to expect. We'll take as few risks as we can get away with. All I know is the longer we stay here, the worse it's going to get."

"You're right. I know you're right." She looked at Wren for a second. "Can we…"

"Can we what?"

"It doesn't matter."

"No, what is it?"

"Can we go back into the garden and do a bit more training?"

Wren smiled. "Course we can."

10

The noise of the second night of partying across at the King's Castle was nowhere near as loud as the night before, but it was enough to drown out the growls of the creatures. Wren and Robyn were in their back garden. They had their newly built incinerator hob in full flame. An open tin of beans was slowly heating in one corner, while a pan of boiling water bubbled in the other. In the centre, a large frying pan was set and four pork sausages were sizzling away, making the girls' mouths water.

Wren reached for the water and brought it off the heat, placing it carefully down on the garden bench.

"Can you keep an eye on the sausages?"

"Course I can," Robyn replied, turning them over with a long barbecue fork.

Wren re-read the instructions on the side of the instant mashed potato packet and poured it over the water, slowly stirring until the mixture began to look like something resembling mashed potatoes. She sprinkled in a little salt before spooning two equal measures onto waiting plates. She then put on a pair of oven gloves, grabbed the tin of beans, which was now beginning to bubble, poured that onto the plates before returning, taking the frying pan off the heat, and placing two perfectly browned sausages on each plate.

"Bon appetite," she said, handing her sister one of the plates.

"I'm famished! This looks great."

"Well, *great* might be a stretch, but at least we can have hot food," she said, raising her glass of orange cordial and clinking it with Robyn's in celebration.

A roar of laughter rose into the air from across the road, and the looks of happiness on both the girls' faces disappeared momentarily.

"We're going to have to go sooner, rather than later, aren't we?" Robyn said.

"Did you look towards the city from your bedroom window today?"

"No. Why?"

"There was lots of smoke, Bobbi. The city's burning and nobody's coming to put it out." The two of them continued eating in silence for a while before Wren spoke again. "If we didn't have them to think about," she said, gesturing in the direction of the party, "I'd say we could stay here a while; train, prepare, get our heads in the right place for this. But they're the X factor. They're unpredictable, we've got no idea what they might do next.. Things might die down and it might be livable, or it could get worse in a heartbeat."

Almost on cue, there was another raucous eruption from across the road.

"I suppose this is what they mean about being stuck between a rock and a hard place," she said, taking another mouthful of mash and beans.

"We just have to be sensible. When the risk of staying here is greater than the risk of heading out, that's when we go."

"That's easy enough to say, but how will we know?"

"Trust me, we'll know."

Suddenly both of them looked towards the back garden gate as they heard footsteps, followed by somebody trying the handle of the front door. There were more footsteps and some giggling before they heard the gate lever, squeaking out of its rest.

"So, this is where you are," Carl said, holding a bottle in one hand while the other one was wrapped around his brother's shoulder. "This is my brother, he's just a couple of years younger than you," he said, nodding towards Wren. "I thought you both might like to come over and join the fun."

The younger brother also had a bottle in his hand. "No," Wren smiled politely, "we're going to bed after supper."

"What, together? We're into that," laughed Carl, and his brother joined in.

"Very funny. Do you have a filter in your brain, or do you just immediately say whatever stupid thing it is that comes into your head?" Wren asked.

Carl's demeanour changed in an instant. He let go of his brother and drunkenly swaggered across towards Wren.

"What did you fuckin' say to me?" he said, grabbing hold of her by the hair, and pulling her head back, causing Wren's plate to fall from her knee and onto the grass.

She grabbed hold of his wrist. "Let go of me, now!"

He pulled her hair back even harder, and she let out a whimper. "Y'see Calum? This is how you need to treat a girl if she won't do what you want her to," he said beginning to laugh.

Wren gritted her teeth, "I said, let go of me."

"Let go of her," demanded Robyn.

Carl started laughing even louder, and his brother, a little nervous, a little excited, started mimicking Carl's laughter.

"Come here Calum, I'll show you how it's done," he said, taking another drink from his bottle.

The younger boy started heading across, but then Wren unleashed a powerful blow with her right fist, and a volcanic spew of blood burst into the air. In the deteriorating light, it looked much darker, but it glistened as it reflected the flames that still flickered from the incinerator.

Calum stopped dead in his tracks, the grin replaced by an open-mouthed look of horror as his older brother let go of Wren's hair and staggered backwards, dropping his bottle and bringing his hand up to his nose at the same time.

Carl looked at his hand as the treacle-like fluid dripped from it onto the lawn. He tried to inhale through his bloody nose, but instead, a spluttering rasp came from the back of his throat. He did not say a word, but suddenly, the ill-intentioned bravado was gone, and it was replaced with a look of pure hatred, as he advanced on Wren.

Carl's fist balled tight as he approached her, but Wren stood her ground. He raised it ready to strike, but Wren unleashed an almighty kick, making direct contact with Carl's testicles. He collapsed faster than a broken deckchair, cupping his hands over his beloved jewels. Tears glistened in his eyes as the flames flickered and for several seconds, he remained immobile, as did his brother, who was frozen in shock.

Everything happened so quickly, and Robyn just watched on, partly in horror, partly in complete awe.

"I'm going to go get my dad," Calum said, and began to run towards the gate, but Robyn quickly blocked his way.

While his back was turned, Wren grabbed her glass of orange cordial, pulled one of Carl's hands away from his groin and threw the contents of the glass onto his jeans before jumping back again and throwing the glass into one of the bushes. As Calum realised he was not going anywhere, he turned back around in the hope his brother had rallied himself.

"Oh my god, he's pissed himself!" Wren said, pointing towards the wet patch on Carl's groin. "Eugh! Gross!"

"That is disgusting. I think I'm gonna hurl," Robyn said, putting her hand up to her mouth.

Calum looked like he was going to start crying. "Get your brother out of here, now. If I see either of you again, the next time you see your balls, they'll be in a jar."

"You...bitch...I'll...get...you for this," Carl spluttered as his brother tried to help him up. He struggled to his feet and Wren unleashed another fast kick, making him let out an audible cry before he crumpled once again.

"Stop it!" Calum pleaded.

"You don't hear too well, Carl. Maybe your nads have got stuck up there in your auditory canal. I told you, I see either of you again, you're going to regret it. Now get out. The pair of you," she said heading across to open the gate.

It was another minute before Carl struggled to his feet again, and his brother helped him out, down the driveway, and across the road. Neither of them said a word. Neither of them looked back in the girls' direction.

Wren watched them as they disappeared from view before shutting the gate and blocking the outside world once again. The two sisters looked at each other and then burst out laughing.

"That was hilarious," Robyn said. "You're my heroine."

"Come here Calum...I'll show you how it's done," Wren said, impersonating Carl's tone. Both girls laughed again.

"I don't think we'll be seeing them in a hurry."

"I wouldn't be too sure; we'd best keep our guard up."

"Seriously? You think he'd come back round after that?"

"Not tonight. He'll be dipping into the freezer hoping he can find a pack of peas that are still half frozen to put on his balls. But he's not the forgiving kind. You can see it in his eyes. His dad's the same. I've questioned his masculinity, his strength. He's lost face in front of his little brother."

"Oh shit!"

"But like I say, Robyn, we keep our guard up."

Robyn looked at her for a while as the meaning of what she said sunk in. "Okay. I'll just make sure I'm always wearing my boots." The two sisters smiled at each other. "Come on," Robyn said, sitting back down on the bench and patting the space beside her. I've got more than enough on my plate for the two of us."

Wren sat down beside her, picked up her fork from the grass and gave it a thorough wipe before the two of them tucked in to the plate of food. They did not speak but just looked thoughtfully into the fire as they ate. When they had finished, they sat back as the flames from the incinerator gradually began to diminish.

"Remember last Christmas when there was a power cut because of the snow, and Dad came out here and fired up the barbecue?" Wren said with a warm smile on her face.

Robyn let out a small laugh. "Yeah, we had steak and sweetcorn for Christmas dinner, 'cos Dad said there was no way his family was going to have cold food on Christmas Day."

"When he came back in, he was like a snowman. His teeth were chattering and all through dinner, he had to have a blanket over his knees, and Mum gave him a pair of her fingerless gloves," Wren said, giggling.

"And then, straight after dinner, the electricity came back on." Both girls laughed. "There isn't anything either of them wouldn't have done for us, Wren."

"I know that."

"Good. It's important. Because at the end…it wasn't Dad. It wasn't Dad who attacked Mum. It was what had taken over him."

"I know."

"I'm your older sister, and If Mum and Dad were here now, they'd be telling us that we have to look after each other. I've been doing a pretty lousy job so far, but I'm going to make it right. I owe it to you and I owe it to them. I loved them so much. And I…I miss them so much." Robyn and Wren began to sob. "I'm going to make it right."

The night air got colder and the flames dampened further in the incinerator. Eventually, the girls began to tire after the events of the previous two days. The adrenalin had long since stopped surging through them and now they began to give in to their weariness.

Wren picked up her plate from the floor, scooped up as much food onto it as she could, and tipped it on the compost pile at the far corner of the garden. "I'm going to call it a night."

"Me too," Robyn replied.

They turned on the small lantern and walked into the house. The pair of them took their dishes into the kitchen, and one wiped them clean, while the other locked the front door and checked the windows.

Happy that the house was secure, the two sisters climbed the stairs, and Wren gave Robyn the lantern. "Night, Bobbi," she said, stepping into her room.

"Night, Wren." She was about to head into her own room but stopped. "Wren!"

"Yes," she replied, popping her head back out.

"I love you."

Wren smiled. "I love you too."

11

Wren used the light button on her watch to see the time. It was one-thirty a.m. Hoots, laughter, and the sound of smashing glass had woken her up. For a moment, she thought it was somebody smashing the windows downstairs, but then she heard it again more clearly and determined it was the sound of smashing bottles.

She heard floorboards creak before the door to her bedroom opened. She remained under her quilt frozen for a second, before Robyn's voice whispered, "Wren? Wren are you awake?"

"What is it?"

"They're stood on the barricade."

"Who?" Wren asked, climbing out of bed.

"There's Carl and his two brothers, and I think there's a woman watching them."

Wren and Robyn opened the curtains a little and looked up the street towards the barricade. Two small fires burnt in metal bins either side, providing them with enough light to see what was going on. The party was still in full swing further down the street as King Donnie held court in his back garden with leftover barbecue and more homemade beer.

"What's he got in his hand?" Wren asked, watching Carl intently.

"I think it's a bottle."

"But what's he doing with it?"

"He'll be drinking, still."

"No, there's something sticking out of it like a…"

"What? Like a what?"

"Oh shit no! He couldn't be that stupid."

"What? What is it, Wren?"

"It's a wick," she said as both of them watched Carl pull a lighter from his pocket and set fire to it. He waited for a moment until the short fuse was burning properly, then he threw it down onto the other side of the barricade.

Neither Wren or Robyn could see what was happening on the other side, but a burst of flame lit up the area for a short time and Carl and his brothers cheered and laughed while the young woman stood on the street clapped excitedly. "You show 'em, Carl. You show 'em," she said, like any drunk watching a fistfight outside a pub on a Saturday night.

The two sisters continued to watch as Carl bent down and picked up another bottle, lighting the wick of that and flinging it into the air and onto the street beyond to more hoots and cheers from his brothers and the female fan club of one.

"Get your clothes on, Bobbi."

"What? Why?"

"Trust me. Get your clothes on." Wren slipped out of her warm and comfy PJs and reached into a drawer to get fresh underwear.

"I don't understand," Robyn said, still standing there, looking out of the window.

"Bobbi. There are bags of garden rubbish, wooden benches, all sorts of things on there that are going to go up like a Catherine wheel on bonfire night the second a flame hits them. There are four transit vans there, all with oil and diesel in them. What do you think's going to happen?"

"Oh no."

"Exactly!"

Robyn disappeared to her room and Wren continued getting dressed, pausing occasionally to look out of the window. She pulled on her socks and then closed the curtains before flicking on her small torch and running downstairs to get her boots. She grabbed two bottles of water from the fridge, knowing there was already some in the bug-out bag, but the more they had the better. She put them by the side of the door and ran back up the stairs to her room, switching off the torch again as she entered.

Robyn was stood back at the window watching. "I think it's okay. I can't see any more flames. I can't see light on the other side."

Wren squeezed in by the side of her sister and they both continued their vigil. A few more minutes passed and the three brothers climbed down from the top of the barricade. Carl staggered and went across to the young woman, falling into her arms. They hooted with laughter and the five of them headed back down the street towards Carl's home. Wren closed the curtains quickly as the raucous, drunken laughter got louder. Then when it finally disappeared, she opened them again.

"There's no one guarding the barricade," Robyn said, looking down the street.

"Like I couldn't have told you that was going to happen."

Wren and Robyn stayed there a while longer, the flames in the two metal bins began to die down, and when the anticipated inferno did not strike, the two sisters closed the curtains once more.

"God, this is only the second night," Robyn said.

"I know."

"We will train again tomorrow, yes?"

"Course we will. We'll keep training until we're sure we can handle ourselves out there."

"I'll see you bright and early then."

"I've got my alarm set for five. Do you want me to wake you?"

"Yeah."

"Cool."

"Cool."

Robyn left Wren's room, closing the door behind her, and Wren cast one more glance out the window before taking off her boots and climbing into bed. She laid there for a while, looking blindly into the darkness before her eyes began to feel heavy once more and she started to drift.

Breaking glass dragged Wren from her dreams once again, but this time it was a different sound. It was not her downstairs window, but it wasn't a bottle, either. She blinked her eyes awake and the room was not as dark as it had been when she had drifted off. She looked at her watch; it was just past two a.m. She could not have been asleep more than a few minutes. She remembered drifting off in the darkness, but now, she could see the basic outline of things in the room as a small amount of light bled in from outside.

She slowly got out of bed, still not sure if she was dreaming. She nearly tripped up over her boots which she had left in the middle of the floor as weariness had enveloped her. She recovered her footing and went to the window, opening the curtains slightly to make sure there was nobody in the street below. When she was certain Carl and his brothers were not outside, ready to hurl something at her bedroom window, she opened the curtains a little wider and looked up the street.

Wren turned and ran out into the hall, bursting into her sister's room. "Bobbi! Get up now! We have to go!" Wren flung the curtains open and her sister, disoriented, struggled with her quilt and climbed out of bed."

"What is it?" she asked.

"We need to go." Wren thundered back out of the room and threw her clothes and boots on.

Robyn was still a little dazed, but instantly jolted back to life when she realised that there was a lot more light in the room than there had been when she'd gone to sleep. She climbed out of bed and went to the window, looking down the street towards the barricade.

"Oh god, no!"

Two of the transit vans were in flames. The debris on top of their bonnets had been consumed by fire. A loud crack sounded as one of the windscreens buckled and splintered with the heat. She looked back down the street to Carl's house. She could see fiery reflections on the wall of their neighbour's house, suggesting their party was still going on and they were all drunk and blissfully unaware of what was happening to the barricade.

"Come on, Bobbi," demanded Wren, returning to her sister's doorway. "We have to go. Now."

"Shouldn't we at least tell them?"

"Screw that. You think they'd tell us? I'll meet you downstairs. Now hurry!"

Robyn quickly put her clothes on, not needing to switch on her torch as the light from the barricade burned brighter and brighter. She pulled on her boots and looked out the window one more time as a drunken couple opened the panelled back garden gate of the Donovan's and began to walk down the path. It took them a minute to fall out of their drunken stupor and realise what was happening. The woman let out a scream and the man staggered back up the path and swung open the garden gate, shouting at the top of his voice.

Robyn looked back down to the barricade. Now, beyond the refuse sacks, the benches and other items that were being reduced to ash, she could see shadows of moving creatures. The flames were licking higher and higher as the fire took a greater hold, burning a huge, inviting beacon to any hungry monsters scouring the suburbs.

Shouts of panic began to reverberate in the street below as the drunken revellers stumbled onto the street to look towards the increasingly ferocious blaze.

"Come on Bobbi!" Wren shouted again, but Robyn could barely tear her eyes away from the unfolding mayhem below. Then it happened, probably what Wren had figured would happen from the point she saw Carl light his first Molotov cocktail. One of the vans exploded as its diesel tank caught fire. A blinding fountain of liquid flames shot through the air like a firework display. The crowd that had gathered in the street suddenly sobered up in a heartbeat and all of them ducked and cowered for a moment as the searing heat whipped through the night air. The mini fireballs splashed on the tarmac of the road, the concrete of the pavements, the bushes and trees in the nearby gardens, and the brickwork of the surrounding houses. In a split second, the scene had turned into something from a disaster movie.

Robyn watched as sparks and lit debris rose higher and higher into the dark sky, and she felt herself become more hypnotised by the moment. She looked back down at the crowd, and she could tell they felt the same. They looked on in abject horror, wanting to move, to stop the infernal tide, but unable to do so; they stood rooted, glued to the spot by their own fear and the inevitability of their own mortality.

"Bobbi. For god's sake. What are you doing up there?"

Her sister's voice broke her out of the trance and she turned, leaving the scene to play out. She ran down the stairs.

"Sorry!" was all she could say as she jumped the last few steps and landed in front of Wren at the bottom.

"C'mon," Wren said, picking up the two water bottles and handing Robyn the two javelins, before heading out into the back garden. She went straight to the shed, opened the bug-out bag, put the extra water bottles in, then took her own javelin back from Robyn. There was enough starlight for them to see what they were doing, and Wren took one of the white plastic garden chairs and put it against the back fence. There was another loud explosion from the street and both girls watched as an eruption of flames shot high into the sky.

"Oh no!" Robyn said, as her eyes followed the fiery arcs.

"Don't worry," Wren replied. "You first." She took the javelin back from Robyn and guided her onto the chair. Robyn grabbed hold of the top of the fence and lifted herself up, placing her foot firmly on the ridge before jumping down the other side and landing upright on the soft ground below.

Wren climbed up, leaned over the fence and lowered the javelins and the holdall down to her sister then jumped up and over herself. The two of them stood there for a moment. The catching flames cast dancing shadows around them, as Wren placed the carry strap of the holdall over her head and shoulder and picked up her javelin. "Let's go," she said, beginning the march across the field.

Robyn remained nailed to the spot for a moment. They had just escaped a desperate situation; was what lay ahead of them any safer?

12

The two sisters made their way across McIntyre's field, occasionally throwing glances over their shoulder towards their home and the street beyond. They could see from their position, that fire had taken hold of the roof of the first house in the street, and the house next to it on the corner of the main road which led onto their street was also in flames.

"This will get out of hand in no time at all," Wren said.

"I think it already is."

"No, I mean *really* out of hand. There's no sign of rain, the ground's pretty dry, no fire engines, no water to fight the flames with. The whole area could go up, thanks to those idiots.

"We'll be out of here by then, won't we?"

"Don't worry. We'll be long gone by then."

They made it to the end of the field, and now they were out of the direct glow of the flames, the pair of them realised it was a little harder to make things out.

"Wren!" whispered Robyn.

Wren stopped in her tracks, as she was about to climb over the fence. "What?"

"I can't see much. Are you sure we should be travelling about in the dark?"

"What are our options?"

"Can we find a safe place for a couple of hours until it's lighter?"

Wren stretched her hands out and gestured around her. "Like where, exactly?"

"I don't know. I just...if there's one of those things out there, it will be on us before we even see it."

Wren climbed back down. "Listen. In the park, the kid's playground, there's that little playhouse thing at the top of the climbing frame and slide. If we can get there, we can stay out of sight until it's morning. Proper morning, I mean."

"Okay."

Wren climbed over the fence, quickly followed by her sister. They both crouched down, taking cover behind the thin interval of trees and bushes that bordered the public park. They allowed their eyes to adjust to the new surroundings for a few seconds then the two of them slowly moved off once again. They kept close together, their arms almost touching. They could feel their eyes widen as their pupils expanded, trying to take in every silhouette, every bizarre shape.

"Do you hear rustling?" whispered Robyn.

"It'll probably be rats or something; don't worry about it."

"*Rats?*"

"Keep your voice down." Wren felt her sister's hand gently grab hold of her arm as they made their way through the park to the centre and the children's play area. "I'm scared, Wren."

Wren stopped and took hold of her sister's hand. "Bobbi, I'm scared too. There'd be something wrong with us if we weren't," she whispered. "But we don't have a choice. We have to do this. Now, come on, stick with me, stay quiet, and we'll be fine."

They did not speak again after that. They walked hand in hand through the park as they had so many times when they were younger. The children's play area had been redesigned a few times since then, finally going all posh when they got a lottery grant to build a new one, but the girls were still just two sisters in the park, like they had been all those years before.

The ground beneath their feet suddenly felt different as they left the grass and walked onto the soft, loose bark chips that coated the ground around the climbing frames, the roundabouts, and the swings. Wren was concentrating hard, trying to make out any unfamiliar shapes, trying to see any wisps of movement that did not belong to the night. She squeezed her sister's hand tight. "This is it," she whispered. "You go first." She guided her sister to the base of the climbing frame and took the javelin from her. "Be careful."

Robyn reached out in front of her until her hands came into contact with the metal rungs of the frame. She slowly climbed until she reached the small, covered section at the top. She leant out of the little circular gap in the treehouse-like structure. "Pass me the javelins," she whispered. Wren slowly raised one, then the other javelin, holding them up until Robyn's exploring hand caught hold of them. Then she climbed up herself. She pulled the holdall from her shoulder and the two of them nestled down into the small gap beneath the javelins, whose ends were poking out of the two circular windows.

"This is comfy," Wren said, as she folded her arms and pushed her hands beneath her armpits for warmth.

"It could be worse." The two of them sat, leaning into each other, listening to the sounds of the night. Then they heard a muffled explosion. "Do you think that's our street?"

"That's my guess. On the upside though, hopefully, a lot of the creatures will head towards the noise and when it's light, they should be able to see the smoke from miles around."

"So, what's the plan?"

"Same as yesterday, but hopefully we'll have a bit more success this time. It's not like we can call this place home if things go bad, is it?"

"I suppose not."

"Try and get a little bit of sleep."

"There's not exactly a lot of room to stretch out."

The two sisters slid down the wall as far as they could and Wren wedged the holdall underneath their heads to act as a pillow.

"Better?" Wren asked.

"Oh yeah, much."

"Sarky cow."

"Eat my farts." The two sisters chuckled before falling silent and gradually drifting into irregular snatches of sleep.

*

Robyn was the first one to open her eyes, and for a while she could not remember the events of the previous evening, or why she was squashed up like a jack-in-the-box, waiting to be freed. Then as she heard her sister's breathing beside her and looked around the cramped interior of the little children's playhouse, it all came flooding back to her. Her neck felt stiff, and she tried to move a little without waking Wren, but it was impossible.

"What time is it?"

"You're the one with the watch," Robyn replied.

Wren wiped her eyes before bringing the watch up to her face. "It's just before five."

"That was a lovely night's sleep."

"Yeah, I feel much better." Wren shuffled up and reached around to the holdall. She unzipped it and pulled out a bottle of water, offering it to her sister first. Robyn took it gratefully and gulped the water thirstily before handing it back to Wren, who did the same. "You want something to eat?"

"Too early," Robyn replied.

Wren climbed to her feet, making sure not to bang her head on the javelins suspended above them through the windows. She stepped out onto the platform of the slide and looked around the park. In the early morning light she could see towers of grey and black smoke drifting into the sky from the direction of their neighbourhood.

"Well, doesn't look like the fire's going out anytime soon."

Robyn shuffled up to join her and the pair of them slowly woke up, watching the last remnants of where they used to live drifting into the atmosphere.

"There's no going back now, but it's going to be a long haul getting up to Inverness."

"I've been thinking about that," Wren replied.

"What do you mean?"

"I mean, maybe it was a bit unrealistic of me."

"You were confident we could do it."

"Yeah, that's back when I thought I had superpowers. Then the first time I came into contact with one of those things, I realised just how unprepared I was."

"What are you saying?"

"I'm saying, I'd hoped I would have had more time to get prepared, mentally and physically. I knew it couldn't last, but I'd hoped we were safe for the time being. But this whole thing happened so suddenly and…"

"And what?"

"Look. We need to get out of the city, that's a given. It's way too dangerous. But maybe we can find somewhere. Maybe you and I can find a place in the country, where we can stay for a while, where we can get to grips with what we're doing. We might even find a car and be able to teach ourselves to drive."

"Where did all this come from, Wren? You were as sure as anything that we'd be fine. That we could make it up to Inverness, no problem. And what about Grandad? You said that if anyone could get through this thing, it would be him. Don't you believe that?"

"Yeah, but that's just the point, isn't it?"

"You've lost me."

"Grandad will do what we're trying to do. Get to a less built-up area. Yes, he's in a place that's tiny compared to Edinburgh, but it's still pretty big. He'll be heading somewhere further out. He'll assume we're gone; why wouldn't he? So, we could travel all the way up there and find out it was a fool's errand. We could get there and find we are no better off than we are here."

"I...I don't know what to say."

"There's nothing to say. These thoughts must have been going around in your head yesterday, too."

"They were," Robyn replied, still watching the smoke in the distance, "But you seemed so sure."

"I was sure, until I had to deal with a murderous corpse head-on."

"You're scaring me now. We're out here. We have no home anymore. We're going to have to deal with those things; there's nothing surer."

"I know," Wren said turning towards her sister, "but the fewer, the better. That's what I'm saying. We might not need to travel half-way to the North Pole to find safety. We might be able to find a cottage or something that we can settle in, just until things calm down. Until we can figure things out."

"Calm down? Do you think things will ever calm down again? I don't know if you got the newsflash, but zombies have taken over."

"Yeah, strangely enough, that fact hadn't escaped me."

Robyn was about to say something else, but just went quiet. The two of them kept watching the smoke for a while before she began to climb down from the small enclosure. "C'mon then," she said, gesturing for her sister to pass the javelins down to her.

Wren passed down the weapons, then the holdall, before finally climbing out of the cramped enclosure herself. She threw the strap to the holdall over her shoulder and the two of them set off towards the far wall of the park. Their heads swivelled every step of the way, looking for any sign of the creatures. Their ears tuned into the sounds of the morning, the wet brush of their feet on the dewy grass, making sure nothing invaded it, making sure no inhuman growls accompanied it.

When they reached the wall, Wren put her hands up against it. They were in the same spot they had climbed over during their first escape. It was the most convenient part of the wall to scale. There were no spiny branches or thorny shrubs to cut themselves on, but there was a part of both girls that wondered and dreaded the prospect of the creatures they had evaded still being on the other side of it. The two sisters looked at each other before gently placing their ears against the cold surface. They stayed that way for more than a minute, desperate to hear nothing but waiting to hear something. When no sound came, Wren tapped gently against the wall, then harder, and then harder still. Still no sound came, so she slid the holdall from her back, leaned the javelin up against the cold black stone and hoisted herself up to peek over the top.

"It's all clear," she whispered, turning her head back round to look at her sister. She climbed onto the ridge properly, straddling it. "Pass me the javelins." Robyn did as she was asked, and Wren took them, leaning them against the other side. "Okay, pass me the holdall." Wren took the holdall, but before dropping it to the floor, removed the carry strap. "Here," she said, lowering one end, "grab onto this, I'll help you up." Robyn wrapped the strap around her wrist and forearm before reaching up to the top of the wall with her other hand. Wren pulled and in no time, Robyn joined her. She released the strap from her hand and smiled, handing it to her sister.

"Thanks," she said.

"No biggie," Wren replied, before swivelling and jumping down the other side. Her sister did the same. Wren reattached the carry handle, picked up her javelin, and the pair of them headed down the embankment. The dense woodland blocked out some of the morning light, but there was enough for both girls to see the felled creature from the other day, still lying there. Robyn and Wren both put hands up to their noses to try and block out the foul stench of decay. They were a few metres past it before the air began to smell like woodland again.

"So where are we heading exactly?" whispered Robyn.

"West. But we need to go north first."

"So, the trading estate again?"

"Yeah."

"Great."

"It shouldn't be as bad. Hopefully, most of them were flushed out when they chased us, and the sound of the bike."

"Yeah, hopefully."

"We'll be able to pick up our rucksacks too. They were well stocked."

"Oh great. I was wondering what was missing from the journey, and that was it, a two-tonne bag strapped to my shoulders."

Wren smiled. "Look, you'll be grateful for those supplies when—"

The creature was already at full tilt shooting towards them through the shadows of the woods before either of them saw it. Wren's breath left her. She stopped dead in her tracks as the gurgling growls took the place of her own words, shattering the otherwise serene calm. She dumped the holdall off her shoulder and locked eyes with the demonic whirlwind.

"*Aaarrrggghhh!*" Robyn screamed, as her eyes followed her sister's. They both raised their javelins simultaneously, as the beast came at them. At two metres back it launched through the air like a pouncing cheetah. Robyn thrust the javelin in its general direction, spiking it through the shoulder, slowing it for the briefest of moments as its body absorbed the impact. Right away the beast tried to regain its footing.

Wren swept her javelin round hard and fast, knocking the creature from its feet and onto its back. Robyn released her javelin. It was buried deep and it whipped out of her hands as the monster fell backwards. The creature immediately began to struggle to its feet, but Wren swiped her javelin hard against its head, dazing it for not much more than a second, but that second was all she needed as she thrust the spear diagonally through the creature's eye.

The struggling stopped instantly and the beast laid there, still, on the forest floor. Wren looked up to see if Robyn's scream had alerted any other monsters to their whereabouts, but for the time being, they were alone.

Wren looked towards Robyn, and her sister returned the gaze as the two of them started breathing again. Robyn pulled her weapon from the slain beast's shoulder. It came out with a slooping sound, which made her feel a little queasy, but there was lots in this new world that made her feel queasy, and she was just going to have to learn to live with it.

"Are you okay?" Wren asked. "It didn't touch you?"

"No. I...I think I'm okay," she said, beginning to examine her clothes and her body. A smile formed on Wren's face. "What are you smiling at?"

"We did it. We killed one...together...as a team."

"I was useless. You killed it."

"What? You weren't useless! You slowed it down, put it off balance. That gave me the chance to knock it off its feet and finish it. We did it together, Bobbi. We'll have to take on more of them, but this is a beginning. We stood our ground and we fought."

"I suppose we did," Robyn replied, wiping the end of the javelin on the clothes of the fallen beast.

"We can do this Bobbi. You and me. We can do this," Wren said before collecting the holdall and setting off once again.

*

13

They crouched down in the same spot they had two days before. They stayed there a few minutes surveilling the area carefully. It all seemed clear, but then again, it had the last time. It was only when the motorbike had sped by that they got noticed.

"Are you ready?" Wren asked, turning to look at her sister.

"Erm, no."

Wren smiled. "We'll be fine. Come on," she said and left the concealment of the shrubbery, stepping out onto the verge.

Robyn let out a long sigh and ran to catch up with her sister. They walked across the dual carriageway, looking in all directions as they went. When they reached the other side of the road, they took the same narrow path they had previously, minimising the risk of them being seen. Then they saw them, untouched as if they had been placed down just a few minutes before...the two rucksacks.

"I was worried these might have been taken," Wren said.

"By who?"

"I dunno, I just worried. I can't believe we're the only people who have been in this area over the last couple of days."

"Maybe not, but, y'know, how many people would have been paying attention to what was in the bushes?"

"Good point."

"Oh no!" A look of sadness adorned Robyn's face.

"What? What is it?"

"I left my phone and the solar charger."

"You expecting a booty call or something?"

"Funny. It had all my music on. It had Dad's...it doesn't matter. It's stupid."

"What's stupid?"

"I was listening to it the other day. I had a load of Queen on there. It made me feel closer to him, that's all."

"I know what you mean," Wren replied. "Music can be funny like that. It can make you think about happy times, sad times.... It can even stop you thinking completely."

"Stupid, stupid, stupid. I'm so angry with myself."

Wren saw her sister was about to cry. She unzipped the end compartment of the holdall. "Good job one of us thinks more than two minutes ahead, isn't it?" she said, handing Robyn her phone and charger.

Robyn's mouth fell open and then tears did come, but they were tears of happiness. She looked at the phone and charger in her hands as if she'd just been given a huge diamond ring looped around Chris Hemsworth's hotel room key. "Wren!" was all she could manage as she threw her arms around her sister and kissed her on the cheek. "You've no idea what this means to me."

"You're my sister, of course I know." Robyn embraced her again, before squeezing the phone and solar charger into her rucksack and putting it on her shoulders.

She picked her javelin up and the two of them walked side by side up that narrow path, each of them taking a handle of the holdall to distribute the weight. They came to the end of the building and ducked down again. Wren peeked around the corner then quickly pulled her head back.

"Is there one of them there?" Robyn asked, seeing the concerned look on Wren's face.

Wren gave a short, sharp shake of her head. "I wish."

"What do you mean?"

"There are about five of them."

"Then we have to go back."

"Go back where, Bobbi?"

"To the woods."

"And do what?"

"Wait."

"We can't just wait in the woods until more of those things stumble across us."

"Then what do we do?"

"Look, if there's one thing I'm good at, it's running. I can get them to chase me, so you can make a break for it."

"That's mad. Don't be stupid."

"No listen, these things aren't bright. They're a bit like Carl and his brothers," she said, trying to make her sister smile, but to no avail. "Okay, maybe they're not that bad, but they won't be too hard to outwit."

"I won't let you. It's a mad idea."

"Staying here is a mad idea. Going back to wait it out in the woods is a mad idea. We need to get to the other side of this trading estate, and then we're through to agricultural land, then things get easier."

"I won't let you do anything so foolish."

"So, what's your plan?"

The two of them crouched down with their backs against the wall, wracking their brains. Then Robyn had an epiphany. "Come with me," she said, and they retraced their steps, then crossed the road to a large showroom on the other side of the trading estate causeway. They kept low and skirted the front of the building, before turning left up the side. There was a narrow ginnel which led to the road the zombies were on. "Okay. Get to the end of here and I'll join you in a minute."

"What? Where the hell do you think you're going?"

"Trust me," Robyn replied. "I won't take any risks."

Her sister disappeared, leaving Wren to struggle with her own rucksack and the holdall, up the narrow passageway. She ducked down again at the end of the building and edged her head out. There was a shallow bank up to some bushes. The road where the zombies were laid just beyond. She shuffled the straps to the rucksack off her back, put the holdall down, and leaned the javelin against the wall before edging up the embankment, ducking down lower and sneaking a look up the causeway towards the five creatures.

They seemed transfixed by reflections of themselves in the dull metal siding of one of the other buildings. Wren had no clue what Robyn's plan was, but the more time that dragged by, the more concerned she became. She looked at her watch. Four minutes had passed since she left.

"What the hell are you up to," she hissed. Another minute passed and Wren belly crawled back down the embankment, picked up her javelin and began to jog back down the narrow ginnel in the direction that her sister had gone.

She was about ten metres from the end when Robyn came running around the corner. "Move...move," she whispered, waving her hands and ushering her sister to change direction. Suddenly, the distinctive opening to Queen's *The Show Must Go On*, began rising into the morning air.

"What the hell?"

"Just get ready to run," Robyn said, as Wren put the rucksack back on her shoulders and the two of them each picked up a handle of the holdall.

They edged up the embankment, but the creatures were already heading down the main causeway towards the sound of the music. Robyn and Wren began to run as fast as they could carrying their rucksacks, javelins and holding a holdall between the two of them. They each threw looks to the left as they passed the road the beasts had run down. The five creatures were chasing down the source of the sound, their backs to the girls.

"What did you do?"

"Never mind," Robyn replied.

They turned right onto the next long causeway that was lined with a mixture of office buildings, showrooms, and storage space.

Wren looked back. "We're still clear," she said.

"Just keep moving," Robyn replied as they followed the road round to the right past more offices before taking a sharp left. The music was well out of range now, but in an instant, it had been replaced by a different sound.

Three creatures were fifty metres away, but their growls were getting louder all the time as they sprinted down the tarmac towards the two sisters. Wren dropped the handle to the holdall and slid the rucksack from her back.

"Oh crap!" Robyn said, slipping free of her rucksack, too, and placing one foot in front of the other to get a good firm stance.

"Crap's right," Wren said, as she suddenly began running towards the beasts.

"What are you doing?!" Robyn screamed, as her sister launched the javelin through the air. The striped spear shot straight like a whistling bullet. It pierced through the torso of one of the beasts, knocking it back off its feet like it had just been hit by a cannonball.

Wren ran back to her rucksack and dragged out the crowbar she had put there two days before. She measured the weight of it in her hand, and as the remaining two creatures approached, she ran again, but this time launched herself, feet first. At the same time, Robyn thrust her javelin forwards, missing her target's head, but having the quickness of mind to sweep the weapon around and knock it off balance.

Wren's feet made contact with the other ghoul square in the chest, sending it cascading backwards. She looked back up the street to see the one she had skewered beginning to struggle to its feet. Without pause, she leapt on top of the creature she had just high kicked and brought the crowbar down on its head, hard and fast, stunning it, then brought the heavy piece of metal down again, and again. The fourth time was the charm. There was a loud crack, causing the filmy grey eyes to snap shut, and rendering the nightmarish monster motionless.

She looked back towards Robyn, who had turned around to deal with the creature she had knocked off balance. It rose to its feet again and lurched towards her. Wren's instinct half-pulled her towards her sister's side, but then Robyn mimicked the move she had seen Wren make in the woods and knocked the creature's feet from beneath it. Before it had a chance to react, Robyn thrust the javelin up under its chin. She felt it cut through layers of tissue before hitting the hard bone of the skull and coming to rest.

Wren turned back to see the first beast gathering pace towards them once more. She began to run towards it, and as it approached, Wren did a sliding tackle, feeling the fabric of her coat rip on the tarmac. The creature, already encumbered by the spear sticking through it, toppled once again, this time onto its side. Its legs kicked out frantically trying to regain footing, but Wren flipped over and unleashed a flurry of deadly blows. Within seconds, the cavernous black pupils retreated into the milky greyness of the creature's eyes and they became nothing but pinpricks absorbing the rising morning sun.

Wren looked across towards her sister, who was standing over the slain creature. She remained there, awash in her own disbelief. Two days before, she would never have dreamed of doing something like this, but now, she had killed one of these things, all by herself.

She turned to look at Wren. "We did it." Robyn walked across and put her hand out, pulling her sister up.

"I knew you had it in you," Wren said.

"You got two, though."

"It's not a competition."

"Come on, we'd better get going, otherwise this will have been for nothing."

The two sisters looked at their handy work one last time. Wren pulled the javelin from the beast she had killed, wiping that and the bloodied crowbar off on its clothes. They put their rucksacks back on, picked up the holdall, and began to jog down the centre of the road once more, towards farmland, towards safety.

14

The two sisters picked up speed as they looked beyond the tall office building at the end of the road, to the car park and the fence. Wren cast a quick glance back to make sure they were not being followed, then allowed herself a small smile.

"We've made it," Robyn said, excitedly.

"We haven't made anything yet," Wren replied, "but it's a step in the right direction."

The pair of them jogged through the entrance and ducked underneath the barrier then continued down the side of the large office block and into the expansive rear car park. It was only as they reached the back fence that their spirits dampened. They slowed from a jog to a walk and eventually came to a complete stop as they dropped the holdall and stepped back. The security fencing in place was about ten feet high. Each single rail was topped off with a sharp triple point on top. It was specifically designed so people could not make it over without causing themselves serious bodily harm.

"Is it okay if I cry now?" Robyn asked.

"Only if I can join you."

Wren took the rucksack from her back and went over to the office building, where she climbed onto a small wall with a bicycle parking rack attached on both sides. From the elevated position she could see that the fence was not just in place for this building, but it appeared to stretch the entire perimeter of the trading estate complex. She jumped back down and went to stand with her sister.

"Well?" Robyn asked.

"It's not good."

"When you say, 'not good,' what do you mean exactly?"

"Erm...bad."

"Okay, can you be a little more specific perhaps?"

"Devastating. Soul crushing. Mortifying."

"So, it's bad then?"

"It's all the way around."

"What are our options?"

Wren walked up to the fence and pushed against it. She wrapped her hand around one of the rails. "Shit!" she hissed. "These things are sharp. We'll cut ourselves to ribbons if we try to climb it." She rested her head against the cold metal and looked through the gap. It was like some cruel joke designed to torture them. There was a small embankment coated with luscious green grass, leading down to a wide drainage ditch. Just beyond was the first of many farmers' fields and the beautiful Scottish countryside, but they could not escape this industrial nightmare.

Wren felt a presence beside her and looked to see her sister staring through the gaps in the fence as well. They were like two prisoners looking out from their cells, knowing they would never be granted freedom.

"Well, we're just going to have to go back out and around," Robyn said.

"We can't do that. There are two big housing estates, one on each side. That was the whole reason we came this way."

"Then what do we do?"

"I don't know, Bobbi, this has only just happened. Give me a minute to think." Wren looked around the car park. It was empty, barring some rubbish and a single flat tyre that someone had obviously changed in a hurry and just discarded. She went up to the entrance door of the office building and tugged on it in the hope that when everybody flew out of the building realising the world had gone to hell, that they'd forgot to lock up. But the door was secure. "Dammit," she said kicking the glass.

She moved along to one of the windows and cupped her hands around her eyes to see in. It was a typical office, furnished with desks, chairs, filing cabinets, computers. Robyn came to join her, and the two sisters stood side by side like the Cratchit family in *A Christmas Carol*, looking at all the toys in the shop window that they could not afford.

"We don't have a choice. We either get past that fence or it's all over," Wren said, stepping away.

Robyn stayed at the window a moment longer. "So what—" her words were cut short as she saw Wren hurling the flat tyre with all her strength at the neighbouring window. The glass imploded with a deafening crash.

Wren quickly wrapped her jacket around her hand and knocked away the errant shards, before climbing in. "C'mon, Bobbi," she said. "Give me a hand."

"What the hell?"

"Just hurry."

Robyn climbed through the broken window. Her feet landed heavily on the glass littered carpet, making the same kind of crunch that they would if breaking through ice. "How is this going to help us?"

"We're going to build a ladder, but we need to be quick. Those things will have heard the crash; they'll be looking for where it came from." Wren tried to drag one of the filing cabinets away from the wall, but it was far too heavy. She flung open the bottom drawer and haphazardly threw all the green hanging files out onto the floor. "Don't just stand there! Give me a hand."

Robyn ran to the next filing cabinet and began to do the same. Wren emptied the final drawer from hers then walked the sturdy metal construction over to the window, before heading out into the hallway and into the next office.

Robyn finished emptying her cabinet and dragged that over to the window, parking it next to her sister's. She ran into the next office and was about to start on another. "No," Wren said as she emptied the bottom drawer of a smaller cabinet. "We only need three. Tear some curtains down, thick towels, fire blankets, anything you can find. Quick!"

Robyn looked toward the windows, but they had Venetian blinds. "Where am I going to find curtains?"

"Just find something Bobbi, we need to cover the spikes on top of the fence."

Robyn ran out of the office and went down the hall, barging through door after door until she found the staff canteen. Rather than the austere looking blinds, the windows were covered with thick, green leaf-effect curtains. She grabbed one end with both hands and dragged them from the tracks as the supporting loops ripped and tore away. Such was her urgency, she was running back out of the canteen within a minute. As she was about to head through the door, she saw a fire blanket attached to the wall. She tugged hard at the release loop and the blanket came free. Not bothering to fold it, she rushed down the hall with it waving behind her like a thick grey cape.

Robyn reached the first office to see Wren climbing back out into the morning sun struggling with a filing cabinet half the size of the others. She rushed to the window, dropping the curtains to the ground, and pushed the top of one of the taller cabinets until it toppled with a

119

loud clatter onto the window ledge. She bent her knees, grabbed hold of the bottom and pushed it upwards, immediately feeling Wren take the weight of it from outside. She dragged it over the ledge, and it landed with another bang, making all the drawers in it judder.

"Okay, the other one," Wren said. The pair of them did the same with that before Robyn threw the curtains out of the window. She climbed out herself and looked at her sister. They both knew they had made a lot of noise that was going to help the remaining creatures, who would in all likelihood have lost interest in the Queen playlist by now, track them down.

"How do we do this?" Robyn asked.

Wren leant one of the filing cabinets towards her and gestured for her sister to lift the other end. The two of them waddled with the heavy piece of office furniture, over the grass verge and towards the fence. "We build a tower. Two filing cabinets at the bottom and the smaller one on top."

Robyn suddenly lost her grip on the smooth edge of the cabinet and it hit the tarmac with a ring that made Big Ben sound muffled. "Sorry!" she cried.

"Just pick it up! Pick it up, Bobbi," Wren yelled.

Robyn grabbed hold of the bottom end of the cabinet once more and the two of them carried it to the fence as fast as they could, dropped it there, then ran back to get the other. "Okay, you take the bottom."

"Whatever," Wren replied, "just hurry." The two of them set off again, and this time, they made it across without any further mishaps. Wren positioned the cabinets back to back next to the fence and moved away to make sure they were level.

"Shit!" Robyn screamed.

"What?" Wren asked.

"They're coming!"

Wren looked across the car park, over the barrier and down the causeway. The five creatures that Robyn had lured away were now heading towards them like freight trains on a downward track.

"Shit!" Wren hissed, running back towards the office. She looked behind her and saw that Robyn was frozen to the spot, still watching the creatures. "Come on, Bobbi! Now!"

Robyn came to her senses and ran after her sister. Wren placed the pile of curtains on top of the smaller filing cabinet and they lifted it in unison, the pair of them did not quite run, but moved faster than it should have been possible for two people to move, carrying such a load. They lifted the smaller cabinet on top of the other two, Wren pulled open the bottom drawer of one of the base cabinets and climbed up. "Pass me the curtains."

Without hesitation, Robyn threw the pile of curtains and the blanket up to her, keeping her eyes on the five creatures that were about to reach the car park barrier. Wren focussed. This was like the closing stages of an eight hundred metre final. *You know your opponent is right on your tale, but you don't risk a misstep by turning to look.* She folded the thick fire blanket in two and placed it over four of the triple spiked rails then grabbed one of the curtains. She folded it in four, making a thick padding, placed that over the same rails, and finally took the last curtain, folded it in two and draped it over the side.

Wren pressed down hard on top of the pad she'd created. There was no way the spikes could penetrate it. Wren turned, to see the creatures were halfway across the car park. Her sister was stood watching. "Bobbi! Quick!"

Robyn jerked back to life and looked towards Wren. She passed her the javelins. Wren dropped one down on the other side of the fence and placed the other just behind her feet. Robyn grabbed one of the rucksacks, but a strap had got tangled with the other, so it was almost as if it was nailed to the ground. She fell to her knees to try to unravel it. "Leave it!" Wren cried, as the creatures continued to sprint towards them.

"But—"

"Get up here!"

Robyn cast a glance to her left to see the beasts were mere feet away. She climbed up onto the tall filing cabinet, then carefully onto the next before lowering herself over the fence, gripping the metal frame with all her strength. She dropped the rest of the way, landing clumsily and rolling down the embankment.

Wren dropped her javelin over the side of the fence and carefully climbed onto the top cabinet; at the same split second, two of the creatures hammered against the bottom ones. The cabinet slipped and Wren immediately lost her footing, but managed to lurch in the direction of the fence. She landed hard on the padded spikes, which did not penetrate the thick covering, but dug into her rib cage. "*Arghh!*" she cried as she heard the top cabinet topple to the ground. She hung there with her legs flailing, desperate to avoid the clutch of the monsters' hands as the rest of the beasts caught up with the pack. She looked down to see her sister gather herself at the bottom of the drainage ditch. Wren felt something bang against her boot, and that's when she gave it one final lunge. She kicked her legs and pulled her body over the padded rails at the same time. Just as the balance tipped and it looked like she was about to plummet the nine feet head first, she grasped the curtain with her left hand, pivoting her body. She swung to the floor, fell, rolled down the hill and knocked her sister's feet from under her.

The two of them lay there for a few seconds. The growls of the creatures eventually made them rally, and they climbed to their feet, looking up the embankment to the arms that were squeezing through the railings, their grey skin shredding on the sharp edges, leaving grisly strips behind. Wren put her hand up to just underneath her chest. "Are you okay?" Bobbi asked.

"I'll have a hell of a bruise there, but I'll be alright."

"We lost all our stuff," Robyn said, sadly.

Wren continued to watch the five creatures, grabbing at the air as if that would pull her and her sister towards them.

"No, we didn't!"

"What?"

"I said, no we didn't," Wren replied, walking across to pick up her javelin.

"We forge our own paths in life, and I will not let these things beat me," she said, climbing back up the incline. She stayed far enough back to keep clear of the grabbing hands but watched them for a moment. This was the first time she had been more or less face to face with these things without the fear of being grabbed or bitten. She looked into their weird grey eyes. She remembered how her gran had developed a cataract in her eye once. It had clouded over, like a marble. It looked like the eyes of these creatures, apart from the pupil. The pupil had vanished behind the cloud in her gran's eye, but here...with these things, it was almost as if the pupils danced on the surface, expanding and contracting like some bizarre, jet black kaleidoscope.

Wren sensed a presence next to her and looked across towards her sister. "We make our own path," Robyn said, and the two of them raised their javelins. They took it in turns to drive the spikes through the creature's eyes, rendering them still in a single thrust. Silence reigned once more and the two girls stood there looking down at their victims through the fence. Wren placed her javelin down.

"Give me a leg up," she said. Robyn cupped her hands low and Wren placed her foot in them ready. "One, two, three!" Wren jumped and Robyn pushed.

Wren threw her arms over the top of the padded fence and shuffled her body up, dragging first one leg, then the second over, then lowering herself down onto the top of the filing cabinets. She sat down and slid off, taking a long look at the fallen beasts, making double sure they were all dead, well, deader than they had been. With a grunt, she lifted the smaller filing cabinet back on top of the others, and with no-one there to help her, it landed with a heavy clunk.

Wren bent down and untangled the strap of the rucksack. She lumbered the heavy bag onto the top of the cabinet pile and climbed up, hoisting it over the top and lowering it down to her sister. She climbed back down and did the same with the second, and finally, the holdall. "There," she said as her sister caught the last bag and placed it on the ground. "We've lost nothing."

Wren began to climb over, taking tight hold of the top curtain's fabric. There was a loud tearing sound and, almost as if it was happening in slow motion, the curtain shifted beneath her and Wren lost her balance, sliding off to the side. She felt a sharp pain and heard a ripping sound as something dug into her stomach. Wren screamed.

"What is it? what's wrong?" Robyn asked.

Wren was in too much pain to speak, and put all her efforts into lifting herself off whatever had impaled her before plummeting to the ground. Robyn caught her as best as she could, and they both fell to the ground. Wren lay cringing in Robyn's arms as the two of them looked down at the bloody wound to the left of Wren's stomach.

"Ow!"

"*Oh shit! Oh shit! Oh shit!*" Robyn almost screamed.

"I think I—" Everything suddenly went black.

•

15

Robyn worked in a supermarket at weekends and during holidays. The work was mundane, but the money was useful for a seventeen-year-old. Now, she thanked her lucky stars as she realised it was going to be one of the best decisions she ever made. The supermarket held regular courses on first aid training. Robyn always said yes, because it meant a day where she could go to college on the company's dime and not have to do a lick of work.

Today, some of that knowledge that she had buried at the back of her head was going to prove useful. When Wren shut her eyes, the first thing Robyn did was check for a pulse. When she felt the steady beat, a wave of relief swept over her.

"I don't know if you can hear me Wren, but I think you're in shock. I'm going to lie you down flat." She placed her sister carefully on her back. "Okay. I'm going to take a look at your wound." Robyn unzipped the bloody coat and lifted Wren's t-shirt. She wasn't able to see much, as the area was covered in blood. Robyn grabbed the holdall; she knew there were a lot more medical supplies in the rucksacks, but she would have quicker access to the ones in the holdall. She reached in, pulling a wad of gauze, bandages, tape and antiseptic cream to the top. Robyn grabbed a bottle of water, unscrewed the top and slowly poured some of it in the area of the wound, washing away some of the excess blood. She could see there was still a significant amount coming out in regular bursts.

"Wren, I'm going to have to apply some pressure to this to see if I can slow the bleeding, okay?" She remembered the woman who had done the first aid demonstration had told her to constantly talk to her patient in a calm and reassuring manner. She reached for one of the packets of gauze and suddenly saw a sealed pair of surgical gloves. "Is there anything you don't think of, sis?" she said, as a loving smile warmed her worried face. She slipped on the gloves and opened two packets of gauze, placing them over the wound and pressing down, firmly. She kept her hands there for a couple of minutes, then threw the bloody gauze to the side and tore open two more, applying the same pressure. Then she remembered. Her tutor had said it took ten minutes for blood to clot.

"Idiot," Robyn said to herself. She kept one hand on the wound and angled Wren's watch around so she could see the face. "Okay...okay, ten minutes." Robyn kept an even pressure and noticed that after three minutes, already the gauze had not absorbed as much blood as before. "It's slowing, it's slowing," she said to herself more than to Wren. At eight minutes, Wren began to rouse. Her eyes blinked open and the first look that crossed her face was fear.

"What's wrong? What's happened?" she asked, her eyes wide in her head.

"It's alright. You got caught on one of the spikes. The bleeding's slowing down."

Wren looked down and saw the discarded red gauze; she saw the bloodied remains of the left side of her jacket and her eyes widened even more.

"I—"

"Don't try to lift your head or speak," interrupted Robyn. "Lie flat and stay still." After eleven minutes, Robyn lifted the gauze. The bleeding had slowed down substantially. "It's looking a lot better than it was. I'm going to put some antiseptic cream on some gauze, and tape over it. Listen, when you were on your hunt for meds, did you find any antibiotics?"

"No. There are some painkillers and ibuprofen."

"Right. We'll give you some of those, but you'll have to have something to eat first." Wren smiled. "What are you smiling at?"

"My sister, Florence Nightingale."

Robyn laughed. "Eat farts, Trophy Girl."

Wren laughed this time. "Ow."

"Serves you right," she said, hunting in the bag for food. She pulled out a tangerine, peeled it and gave it to her sister. "Eat this while I find something else, and watch out for pips." Wren did as she was told. Robyn took out a packet of boiled ham and a small tin of pineapple rings. "Here we go, breakfast of champions," she said, peeling open the packet and handing Wren a slice of ham.

The two sisters ate in silence, occasionally looking around them. Despite the dire nature of their situation, both of them felt remarkably lucky to be there. It was hardly a picnic, but they devoured the ham and the pineapple chunks before taking it in turns to drink the sweet juice from the tin. By the end of the meal, a little colour had returned to Wren's cheeks.

"Thanks, Bobbi."

"For what?"

"You saved my life."

"Hardly. It wasn't that deep."

"Yeah, but if you hadn't been here, I'd have bled out."

"I was just repaying the favour. How many times have you saved mine since yesterday morning?"

"This isn't about who does what; it's about both of us getting to safety. You and me...as a family."

Robyn gently brushed the hair from her sister's brow. "Let's get you those tablets sorted out," she said, reaching back into the holdall. She gave her sister the bottle of water and lifted her head slightly so she could take the four tablets. "We'll give it a few more minutes, then do you want to try standing?"

"I'll stand now," Wren replied, eager to get off her back.

Robyn placed a hand on her shoulder. "No!"

"We wait a few minutes, then we'll give it a try."

After a few minutes, Robyn carefully helped Wren to her feet, Wren stumbled a little at first, but quickly righted herself, putting her arm around Robyn for stability.

"I'm alright," she said, eventually letting go of her sister."

"Here, take this," Robyn said, handing Wren a javelin. "I think we're going to have to dump one of the rucksacks. There's no way you can carry it in your state."

"I'll be fine."

"Don't be stupid, Wren. No you won't."

"We can't dump a whole rucksack, not out here. That could be the difference between life and death."

"And what would you call it if your wound opened up due to the strain of too much weight and I couldn't stop it next time?"

"Which is the one with the best supplies in?"

"They've both got different things in. Look, maybe we could get rid of a bit of the stuff, redistribute it, then I could still carry some. How would that be?"

Robyn thought about it for a while. "Okay, but I'm serious, you can't take too much strain."

"Okay, give me a minute."

They placed the two rucksacks and the holdall on the floor and Wren spent the next ten minutes repacking. She discarded some t-shirts, a pair of jeans, a map book and various other items, putting a few more into Robyn's rucksack. She tested the weight and offered it to Robyn. "Right, fair enough, but if you feel anything we stop straight away, yeah?"

"Yeah."

Her sister helped Wren get the much lighter rucksack onto her back before she placed her own, much heavier rucksack onto her shoulders and picked up the holdall too. They began their journey across the field, slowly at first, as Wren got used to walking with her injury.

"So, have you had any more ideas on where we're heading?" Robyn asked.

"Not yet, but the more distance we put between ourselves and this place, the happier I'll be."

"Me too."

The two sisters walked side by side, stopping regularly for water and toilet breaks. The countryside was quiet. They walked through fields rather than followed roads and Wren kept checking the compass to make sure they were keeping to a westerly course. They kept looking back to see the huge trading estate disappearing to nothing on the horizon. The sun was high in the sky when they stopped for lunch.

Robyn checked the gauze on Wren's wound to see if they had absorbed much blood, but it seemed the worst of it was over. They ate an orange each, shared a tin of cold baked beans, and finished it off with two Oreos a piece.

"Lunch of champions," Robyn said, with a smile on her face.

"You're not going to say that after every meal, are you?"

"Dunno. Might do."

"We need to start looking for a place."

"What do you mean? It's only early afternoon."

"Yeah, but we don't want to pass by a decent place only to find ourselves trapped outside when it gets dark. It's not like we can call a cab or something is it? Especially with me the way I am."

"What sort of place?"

"I don't know, anywhere that looks safe where we can get a night's sleep without being worried about being attacked if one of those things wanders past us."

The two of them sat in silent contemplation for a while looking off into the distance where huge plumes of smoke decorated the Edinburgh skyline.

"Well, I suppose we'd better get going then," Robyn said. They picked up their javelins and their rucksacks. Robyn flung the strap of the holdall over her shoulder, and they set off once again. They passed through another gate, and then Wren caught sight of something. She stopped.

"That's a steeple."

"Huh?" Robyn replied.

"Over there," Wren said pointing just above the tree line.

"What do you think we should do?"

"Well, if there's a church, there's going to be a village or something nearby. We might be able to find somewhere to bed down for the night. We'll carry on a bit then we'll check it out. Do a bit of covert surveillance."

"Oh yeah, with me carrying a rucksack and a holdall, and you with a big hole in your stomach? We'll practically be camouflaged."

"Arse!"

"Bitch!"

"Cow!"

"Fart-face!"

The two sisters laughed, but they both knew it was just bravado. When people were turning into flesh-eating monsters left right and centre, the last place anybody should think about going is where there were more people. But right then, right there, they realised that the well containing all their options had run dry.

16

Robyn and Wren had dumped their rucksacks behind a dry-stone wall before settling down for a long vigil in the tall grass. The sun was beating down, but the oak trees lining each side of the lane provided them with enough shelter from its rays. The midges, though, were another matter. Robyn applied a second layer of repellant spray.

"I'd forgotten what these little shits were like."

"They're always worse out here," Wren replied.

Robyn put the canister back in her jacket pocket and nestled back down into the grass. They had been watching the church for over twenty minutes and not seen a sign of anyone. They could just make out a small village street beyond the walls of the churchyard. The church itself looked steeped in history, with its black stone walls and tall, proud steeple. It was from another time, and from what they could see of the street beyond it, that was too.

"How long are we going to wait before we go take a look?"

"I suppose we've waited long enough. There hasn't been a single soul. Come on," Wren said, rising carefully to make sure her wound did not stretch.

"Shall we leave our stuff here, just in case?"

"I don't think so. I think we should take it with us. If we run into trouble, we might get cut off. We might have to head another way."

"I suppose," Robyn replied, climbing back over the wall and pulling the heavy rucksack onto her shoulders. She passed Wren the other one, as well as one of the javelins, before picking up her weapon and the holdall.

"I wish you'd let me help with that."

"Hopefully we're going to find somewhere to hole up for the night. We can get some rest, redress your wound, and maybe tomorrow you'll be in a better state to carry a little more."

"I'm okay to carry more now."

"Stop being so stubborn, Wren. We can't risk your wound opening up again, or we're back to square one." Robyn climbed back over the wall and the two sisters headed up the road towards the church. Any other day, and this would have been like a holiday. A gentle breeze blew warm air against their backs, guiding them towards the serene village up ahead.

They reached the stone wall surrounding the churchyard, and saw there was a large cemetery which ran all the way up one side, and disappeared around the back.

"That's a big cemetery for a small village," Wren said.

"What you've got to remember is when you start getting into the country, the churches are like the schools. They serve a big area."

"I suppose."

The two of them walked alongside the wall, constantly looking around for movement. They could see more of the street beyond now. There were a few buildings lining either side of a narrow road. They could make out the sign on the first of them, it said: "General Store." Robyn unlatched the black wrought iron gate that led into the church grounds.

"Let's see if anyone's at home."

"Why? Don't we want to just find somewhere to bunk down for the night?"

"Well, yeah, but this place is as good as any."

"How do you figure?"

"It's quiet, there's a wall all the way around it, and if it turns out the minister is still alive, he's not going to turn away two of God's children in their time of need, is he?"

"I suppose," Wren said, as the two of them walked through the gate and headed up the pavement towards the church entrance.

Robyn was about to open the heavy, dark oak door when Wren caught sight of something. It was a figure running towards them from the street.

"Quick," Wren said. "There's one of those things coming."

"So much for it being a quiet village," Robyn replied, pulling down the ornate handle. As she opened the door a scream ripped through the air.

"*Nooo!*"

A look of confusion swept across Wren's face; the call had come from the creature sprinting towards them, which had now stopped dead in its tracks on seeing that the door was swinging open. Wren turned to look as the gap widened and her face turned as pale as Robyn's when they saw the throng of creatures that had once been the congregation storming towards them.

Robyn was frozen, but Wren pushed the door shut again as hard and as fast as she could just as the first of the beasts battered their bodies against it. Even through the thick wood, her hands jumped with the force. The two sisters backed away from the door, keeping their eyes firmly fixed on it, making sure nothing escaped the confines of the church. They continued down the path in reverse for several metres before turning and running. They left the churchyard and closed the gate behind them, giving one final look towards the entrance, before heading towards the man who had tried to warn them.

The figure remained there in the street, his head going back and forth like he was at a tennis match. He looked towards the girls, then back to the church, then at the girls, then back at the church again. As Wren and Robyn reached him, they saw he was dishevelled looking, in his forties, with thin black greasy hair and a belly that protruded from underneath the stained, grey tank top he was wearing. "I tried to warn you," he said.

"Thanks," Robyn replied.

"What are you doing here?" he asked, looking at the javelins the girls were carrying.

"We were looking for somewhere to rest. My sister got hurt."

The stranger looked towards Wren and back to Robyn. "Two pretty young girls shouldn't be out alone with this sickness infecting people."

"Erm, I think it's a bit more than a sickness," Wren replied.

"Hmm," he said, scratching his chin. "Well, I suppose you could come to my place to rest."

"That's really kind, but we don't want to trouble you; you've already helped us enough," Robyn said.

"It's no trouble. I...I insist."

Robyn looked towards Wren, who had her hand over her wound and was looking down at it. "Are you okay?" Robyn asked.

"I think it might have opened up again," Wren replied apologetically. "When I pushed the door, I felt something tear a little."

The man looked down at Wren's bloody coat. "What happened? Were you bitten?"

"No, I got caught on some fencing."

"I don't have much in the way of medical supplies, but it looks like you could do with some time off your feet."

Robyn looked again at Wren, then back at the stranger. "Okay...thank you. If it's no trouble."

"No, it's no trouble." The man smiled revealing a mouth full of yellow teeth, "It will be nice to have company. Let me take that for you, you're carrying enough," he said, reaching for the holdall.

"Where's everybody else?" Robyn asked, as the three of them started walking down the centre of the street.

"Everybody else?" the man asked. He shook his head sadly. "They're all in the church."

"How come you weren't there?" Wren asked.

"I was...late. When I got there, I saw what you saw. The minister wanted a village meeting," he said, pointing to a small poster in the window of an accountant's office.

"You were lucky then, Wren said."

"You could say that."

They continued down the street in silence and Robyn kept looking at Wren, who seemed to be holding her wound tighter.

"Is there a doctor's surgery, or a chemist, here?"

"There's a doctor's. There's a small dispensing chemist, but I told you, everybody's gone."

"Yeah, but where is it?"

"It's at the end of the street. Just set back from the road a little. I..."

"You what?" Robyn asked.

"It...doesn't matter."

The three of them continued, and when they got to the end of the street, the man pointed in the direction of the surgery, before turning in the other direction and heading onto a narrow lane. "Where are we going?" Robyn asked.

"I told you. I'm taking you to my house."

Robyn and Wren looked at each other. "Is it far?" Robyn asked.

"Not at all," he said as they continued up the track. They came to a break in the trees and bushes on the left-hand side, and the man opened a white gate whose paint was badly chipped. "That's my house," he said, pointing up the to a small white cottage that had black water stains as a result of broken guttering. "Home sweet home," he said, leading them to the door. "You wouldn't mind leaving those out here would you?" he said, gesturing to the javelins. There's not really a lot of room for them in the hall, it's quite narrow." The two girls shot each other concerned looks as their host opened the door, releasing a wave of warm, stale air. "Excuse the mess," he said as they stepped over the threshold. The door opened into a cramped, dimly lit hallway that was made even darker by striped, bottle-green wallpaper interspersed with thin gold and black stripes.

Their host slipped his shoes off, and he paused, looking at them, expecting them to do the same. They looked down at the dirty beige carpet and struggled not to show disgust on their faces as they kicked off their boots and flicked off their rucksacks. "I'll get the kettle on," he said, walking down the hall and into the kitchen. Wren and Robyn looked at each other, shrugged and followed him. They stepped into the kitchen and their noses immediately twitched at the smell. There were mouse droppings on the floor, and a trap had sprung in the corner. There was a small wet patch around the dead rodent and the odour suggested it had been there for days.

"Erm, actually, I'm not that thirsty," Robyn said.

"No, me neither. In fact, I'm feeling quite a bit better than I was. I think that walk did me good," Wren added.

"Well fresh air always makes me thirsty, so I'll have a cuppa anyway," he said, placing the kettle on the solid fuel range. "Go through to the living room, I'll be in directly."

"Where's the living room?" Robyn asked.

"Stupid me," the man said, pushing past the two girls and stepping back into the hall. "Here, make yourself at home." He opened the first door on the left and stayed there. The girls brushed past him and walked in. "I won't be a minute," he said, retracing his steps to the kitchen.

"We've got to get out of here," Wren said.

"I know. Look, we'll let him finish his tea, and then thank him and go find another place. If the whole village is in that church, there must be plenty of free houses," Robyn said, as the two of them sat down on the 1980s floral design sofa. There were two matching armchairs and, like the hallway and the kitchen, the place smelt rank and looked like it hadn't been cleaned in years.

"The sooner the better. I think the wound's bleeding again."

"Shit! Look. When we get out, we'll head to the doctor's, get some proper supplies."

Their host started whistling in the other room. "There's something really weird about that guy," Wren said. "And did you smell him? The water's only been off a couple of days, not a couple of years."

"I know...I suppose we could just slip out, while he's making his tea."

"That's easier said than done. The door's wide open, we'd need to get our boots on, our rucksacks, there's no way. He'd see us. Look. Let him finish his tea. We thank him again, then go."

"Okay." They sat there, perched on the end of the cushions, not wanting to sit back in the filth encrusted sofa.

Their host came back through the door with his mug, and rather than going to sit on one of the free armchairs, plonked down, just a few centimetres away from Robyn, making her shuffle up even further towards her sister.

"Anyway, I'm Norman," he said, smiling.

"I'm Robyn, and this is my sister, Wren."

"Pretty, pretty girls the two of you."

There was an uncomfortably long pause before Wren replied, "Thank you."

"So, what were you doing in the village? How did you see us?" Robyn asked.

"I caught sight of you from the window," he replied, taking a drink from his mug.

"Erm, how? You can't see the church from here," Wren said.

"Oh, silly me. Yes, I was at my house," Norman replied.

"I thought this was your house," Robyn said.

"Well, it is. This is where I grew up. It was my mum's house, and now...it's mine. Mum was in the church when..."

"So, you have two houses? Why didn't we go to the one nearer the church?"

"Oh no, no, no. We couldn't do that. That wouldn't be a good idea," he said putting down his mug on the coffee table and standing up. "Would either of you like a biscuit? I've got custard creams or digestives."

"No. You're fine," Robyn replied. She waited until he was out of the room and immediately stood. "Come on. This guy's a whacko—I'm guessing his surname is Bates. We need to get the hell out of here now."

"Agreed," Wren said, getting to her feet. They heard tins being opened in the kitchen and both of them crept out of the room and down the hall. They slipped on their boots quickly and quietly. Robyn helped Wren to put her rucksack on, and was just about to put her own on, when Norman came back out of the kitchen. He stopped in mid-stride, holding four custard creams in one hand and the mouse from the trap in the other.

"What are you doing?" he asked calmly.

"We're going," Robyn said, staring at the dead rodent dangling by its tail. "We've decided to head on to the next village before nightfall, so we need to get off."

"I see," he said. "That's a bit rude, don't you think? I offer you hospitality and you get up and head out the second my back is turned."

"I'm sorry," Wren said, "but we need to get going…our Grandad's expecting us and…we don't want to get caught outside in the dark."

"I thought you were going to rest here. I thought that was the plan," he replied.

"I'm feeling a lot better," Wren said.

"Well, you don't look it. You're looking a little pale and clammy," he said, carefully putting the biscuits down on the telephone table and balancing the furry little corpse on top of them. Norman began to walk towards them. "You should stay here until you're feeling better. I have plenty of room."

"No, you're fine, thanks," Robyn said, putting her rucksack on, and picking the holdall up.

Wren tried the door handle, half expecting it to be locked, but when warm fresh air rushed into the entrance, relief enveloped her. "Thank you again," she said, almost running out, and grabbing her javelin.

"Yeah, thanks Norman," Robyn said, grabbing her javelin as well. The two girls speed-walked down the path and out of the gate. They cast a glance back towards the doorway to see Norman still stood there, watching them with a bemused look on his face. Once they'd turned and started up the narrow lane towards the village, both of them let out a deep breath.

"Wow!" Wren said.

"That was the creepiest guy I have ever met, and trust me, I have met an awful lot of creepy guys in my time."

"Didn't stop you bringing them home though, did it? Slapper!"

"Virgin!"

"Prozzie!"

"Old maid!"

The two sisters let out a small laugh before Wren moved her hand back to her wound.

"I'm sorry, I'm really going to have to rest up."

"It's okay, sis. We'll find somewhere."

17

It did not take Robyn and Wren long to get back to the main street in the village. They had deliberately walked in double-quick time, more than a little concerned that creepy Norman was following them.

"He said the doctor's surgery was this way," Robyn said, and the two of them veered onto a path by the side of what looked like an old schoolhouse. There, at the end of the path was a small sign that said "Surgery Parking." The surgery itself was a large stone-built building that fitted in with the rest of the village. At one time it had probably been the home to some very well-off merchant. The pair of them walked through the car park and up the front steps. Wren reached out and twisted the grapefruit-sized brass doorknob, but to no avail.

"I'm guessing that means they're closed," she said stepping back from the door.

"We'll go take a look around the back." They walked around the sizeable detached building, passing windows with Venetian blinds up, until they reached a small, high, frosted glass window. Robyn bent down and picked up a large stone, then proceeded to smash the glass out of the window. She made sure to wipe all the jagged shards from the sill, dumped her rucksack on the ground, placed her hands inside the frame and jumped up, pulling herself through, head first. Her body, then her feet, disappeared from view, but within a minute, she had re-emerged through the large wooden door at the rear of the surgery. She collected her rucksack, javelin, and the holdall, before taking hold of Wren's arm and guiding her in.

Robyn locked the door behind them, and they piled into the first examination room they came to. The two sisters placed their javelins against the wall, unhooked their rucksacks once more, and Robyn dumped the holdall in the corner. There was an alcohol hand wash attached to the wall, and both girls pressed the dispenser button to coat their palms with a healthy layer of the cool gel. They massaged it into their skin thoroughly.

"Take your jacket off, Wren. Lie down on the examination table. I won't be a few minutes," Robyn said, heading back out of the room.

Wren did as she was instructed. She took her jacket off then lifted her t-shirt to see that the gauze was saturated and blood had leaked all over her skin. She put her hand up to her forehead and brought it back down with a sheen of perspiration on her fingers. She was feeling hot and sweaty, and she hoped that was due to the blood loss and exertion and not an infection. She pulled her t-shirt off and went to lie down on the examination couch. Despite the warmth of the day, she began to feel a little chilly, so folded her arms across herself to try and warm up. When Robyn had still not returned after five minutes, Wren started to get concerned and struggled down from the examination table. She looked back at the blue lining sheet; there was a dark streak down the middle of it where perspiration from her back had soaked it.

"That's not good," she said as she headed towards the door. Outside in the wide hallway, there was no sign of Robyn. There were a number of doors and a staircase leading up to a second floor, but there was no sound to give her a clue as to which direction her sister had gone. "Bobbi?" she shouted, but there was no reply. "Bobbi?" she called louder this time.

An uneasy feeling came over her, and she slipped back into the examination room to grab her javelin. She headed back out into the hall and slowly went from room to room. At the end of the hall to the right was a reception desk and the waiting area. There were posters up on the wall like there were in any doctor's surgery. *Have you had your flu jab? Can you spot the signs of dementia? Heart Disease: The Silent Killer.* There was nothing out of the ordinary, but Wren's heart began to race.

"Bobbi!" she shouted again. This time she heard a sound from upstairs. It was a loud thud, like a body falling to the ground. "*Bobbi?*" she whispered.

Wren walked back down the hallway and slowly began to climb the stairs, holding the javelin out in front of her. The building had tall ceilings, and there was a small landing half-way up before the stairs double backed on themselves. She could feel her wound stretching with each step she took. The perspiration began to run down her face, but she still felt chilly. She heard another thud, and despite the pain and discomfort, she started moving faster.

Wren reached the top landing and stood there looking at the four closed doors. She had no way of telling which room the sound had come from, and she did not want to risk shouting again. Her grip tightened around the javelin as she eased open the first door. It was a small stationery cupboard. She opened the second door, and the smell of fresh paint hit her straight away. Decorator's sheets covered the carpet and a step ladder stood in the middle of the room. Wren moved onto the next room which was an office. There was a desk over by the window and filing cabinets lined the walls. She felt the sweat running down her back as well now, and no matter how hard she tried to grip the javelin, she felt it was not hard enough, as if her strength was leaving her. Despite this, she wrapped her hand around the handle of the last door and pushed it open, running into the room, spinning around, ready to attack.

"What the hell are you doing?" Robyn asked, as Wren stood in the middle of the room, in her jeans and bra, waving her javelin around hopelessly.

"I heard...I thought...you were in trouble."

"I was getting supplies. They've got all sorts here. God, Wren! You look terrible." Robyn went up to her and felt her sister's forehead. "You're red hot."

"I feel cold."

"You're running a fever. I've found some antibiotics—amoxicillin—we'll get your dressing changed, get some painkillers and anti-inflammatories down you and we'll stay here the night." Robyn picked up a small box that she had put all the supplies in, took the javelin from her sister, and led her out of the room. "Walk behind me. Hold on to the bannister. You look like you could pass out any second."

"I thought you were in trouble. I heard a thud. I thought you were in trouble."

"I was shifting boxes around up there. Some of those things weighed a ton."

"I was worried," Wren said and she paused on a step for a second.

"What is it?" Robyn asked, looking concerned.

"Bit light-headed."

"We're nearly there, just take it slowly. Put your hand on my shoulder if you want to."

Wren put one hand on her sister's shoulder and the other on the bannister until the pair of them reached the ground floor.

"Feel dizzy."

Robyn put the box down on the ground and took a tight hold of her sister's waist, practically carrying her back to the examination table Wren had been lying on a few minutes before. Wren had deteriorated quickly, and now, she could not even manage to climb onto the high table. With some difficulty, Robyn managed to manoeuvre her on before she went back out to collect the box.

When she arrived back in the room, tears were running down Wren's face. Robyn put the box down on the doctor's desk and rushed to her sister's side, stroking the damp hair from her forehead. "What is it?"

"I...I was scared when I heard that thud. I thought that something had happened to you."

Robyn bent down and kissed her sister on the cheek. "And even despite all this," she said, gesturing towards Wren's wound, "you came to rescue me." Robyn smiled.

"I don't feel very well, Bobbi. If anything happens to me, I just want you to know I love you."

"Nothing's going to happen to you, silly. And I already know. We're sisters, remember? Now, just forget about everything. Relax, and take these," she said, unscrewing a water bottle, putting some tablets in her sister's mouth and easing her head up so she could take a drink. She took five tablets in all. Robyn gently lowered her head back onto the table. "Good. I'm going to take the tape off. It's going to hurt a bit."

"That's okay, just do it."

Robyn pulled the tape off, bringing the blood-soaked gauze with it. She could not help but curl her nose a little at the gooey mess underneath, and she cast a quick glance towards her sister in the hope that she had not seen her expression. Thankfully, Wren had her eyes closed. She just wanted it to be over.

"I'm going to clean it with alcohol. I won't lie to you, this will hurt."

"*Aaarrrggghhh!*" Wren screamed.

Robyn cleaned the wound and all the surrounding area. The bleeding had more or less stopped, but it was clear that any activity could open it up again.

"I found a couple of boxes of butterfly stitches. They're not ideal; you could probably do with sewing up properly, but they're the best we've got right now." Robyn opened the box, took out four of the specialist plasters and removed the non-stick paper. She carefully stretched each of the plasters over the wound, bringing the edges of the cut as close together as she could before placing another gauze over the top and finally, some more medical bandage tape. She looked back at her sister's face. Wren still had her eyes closed. "That's it. We're done."

Wren squinted down at the neat dressing. "You should be a nurse."

"No thanks," she replied, walking across to Wren's rucksack. She unfastened it, and brought out a fresh t-shirt. "Did you bring a sweater or something?"

"Didn't think I was going to need one."

Robyn reached into her own rucksack and searched around, eventually pulling out her favourite comfy jumper. "Here," she said walking over to her sister. "You need to stay warm." She handed her the t-shirt and helped her to sit up. She put her hand on Wren's back and immediately recoiled. Her skin was still hot and clammy. "You've definitely got a fever."

"You still happy for me to wear your favourite top?"

Robyn smiled. "Just make sure you have it dry cleaned before you give it back to me."

Wren put the fresh clothes on. "What now?

"What now, is, I go find some blankets or whatever, we get you cosy, and you rest. An afternoon's rest and a good night's sleep will help you."

"Sorry, Bobbi. This really screws our plans up."

"Don't be stupid. If you hadn't gone back over for our stuff, we wouldn't have food to eat, we wouldn't have a change of clothing or anything. Now, lie down and rest. I'm going to prop the door open. If you need anything, shout me."

"Thanks," Wren said, holding out her hand. Robyn took it and squeezed. "Love you, sis."

"You're really starting to freak me out with that. Let's just take it as a given from now on," she said with a smile. Robyn disappeared into the hall and came back a few minutes later with a couple of thin blankets, half a dozen clean towels, and two coats. "Well, it's not ideal, but hopefully, they'll keep you warm," she said, carefully laying out the assortment of items on top of Wren, and tucking her in tightly. "Now try and get some sleep."

"Where are you going to be?"

"I'm going to block the window in the downstairs loo, and have a look around the place." Robyn made sure the examination table was pushed right against the wall and the brakes were firmly locked before she headed out. "Have a nice nap," she said. She went out into the hall and straight to the small cleaning cupboard she had seen earlier on. She took out a dustpan and brush and headed into the downstairs toilet where she proceeded to sweep up all the broken glass. She looked at the gap in the window. She didn't have any real tools as such, but she would do what she could.

Robyn had not said anything to her sister, but she was concerned about Norman tracking them down. There was definitely something wrong with that guy, and the fact she had specifically asked where the doctor's surgery was, gave him more than a small clue as to where they might head.

It had never been Robyn's intention to stay here, just to get what they needed, and then find somewhere else, but Wren was weak, and she needed rest, and to do that in a place full of medical supplies was not such a bad idea. Robyn headed back down the hall to reception. She walked behind the counter and pulled out a tape dispenser and a pair of scissors. There was a large cardboard box in the corner that was still half full of new lever arch files. She emptied them out and took the box with her down the hall, dropping back into the cleaning cupboard and collecting a couple of black plastic refuse sacks, on the way. She held the box up to the toilet window and started cutting out a piece of cardboard to cover the gap. When she was done, she wrapped the cardboard in the plastic bags and used half a roll of tape, securing it to the UPVC window frame. It was suddenly very dark in the small toilet, the only light coming in was from the corridor outside.

Robyn walked back down the corridor and into each of the examination rooms. On the walls were a number of framed certificates for the doctors and other health professionals who worked there. She collected more than a dozen all told before making her way back to the toilet. She leant them carefully against the window. If anyone tried to gain access, there would be an almighty clatter announcing their arrival. Robyn gave her work a nod of approval then went to explore the small kitchen. She opened the cupboards to see half-opened packets of biscuits, as well as coffee and tea. Everybody probably brought their own lunches; it was not as if the small village had a plethora of takeaways or other places to eat. Robyn picked up a packet of chocolate digestives and started snacking on them as she casually stepped back out into the reception and waiting area.

She sat down in one of the cushioned chairs and began leafing through a pile of magazines. As her stomach began to fill, her eyes got weary, and she slowly drifted off to sleep.

18

"Bobbi! *Bobbi!*" was the scream that jolted Robyn from her nap. The magazine fell off her knees as she jumped to her feet and ran down the corridor to the examination room.

"What is it?" she yelled, storming into the office with one fist clenched, ready to fight.

Wren looked at her in a daze. "I...I had a nightmare and you weren't here."

"Jesus, Wren! I thought something had happened."

"It was horrible. That guy had come for us. He'd tied me to the table and carried you off."

Robyn looked annoyed for a second that she had been awakened in such a startling manner, but then she softened. "Well, yeah, I suppose that would make me scream too. Look, it's okay. We're safe in here," she said taking her sister's hand. "The doors are locked, I blocked up the window, and if anybody tries to get in, I rigged an alarm system." She reached across and felt Wren's head. "Your fever seems a little better." She looked at Wren's watch. "Wow. That was quite a nap. Another hour and you'll be able to take some more tablets. I'll start making something for us to eat."

"Please not cold beans again."

Robyn smiled and delved into the rucksack for the small camp stove and pan. "No, we can do better than that. How do you fancy an M&S curry?" she said, pulling out a tin and some couscous."

"That sounds a lot better than what we have been eating."

"You need to keep your strength up, plus you need to have food in you to take your tablets. How are you feeling...in yourself?"

"I feel less light-headed, less…clammy."

"That's good," Robyn replied, heading back out of the door.

"Where are you going?"

"I'm going to the kitchen so I can use the stove without fumes building up in the room. I'll just get the water on for the couscous, then I'll come back in."

"I'm sorry I scared you."

"It's okay, Wren. You were running a fever, you're taking tablets, it's only natural you have weird dreams."

"I like us like this."

"What do you mean?"

"I mean...like this. Looking out for each other."

"I was a pretty lousy older sister, wasn't I?"

"You were just an older sister. I know a lot worse."

"Well from now on, it's you and me. We're all we've got, and I'm going to look out for you, and I know you'll look out for me." Robyn immediately put a finger up to her lips. "Don't say it," she said, and they both smiled.

They ate well, they talked, Wren took her medication, and as night crept in, Robyn lit a few candles she'd found along with a torch under the receptionist's counter. Wren had the foresight to pack a deck of cards, and the two of them played like the old days when they went on camping trips with their mum and dad. It was past eleven when Wren began to drift again. Robyn packed everything away, wheeled an examination table in from the next office, put on her jacket, zipped it up and curled up for the night.

*

Robyn felt a hand over her mouth and a blade against her neck. Just from that horrific smell, she knew immediately who it was, but for the life of her, she could not understand how he had got in without triggering her booby trap. "Don't say a word, pretty, or both of you die," whispered the voice. Robyn looked across at her sister, who was still doped up and fast asleep, and in that one moment, she wanted to warn her more than anything, but she knew that warning would cost them both their lives.

Robyn stayed silent as she climbed off the examination table. Norman took his hand from her mouth and instead grabbed a fist full of her hair, while still keeping the blade to her neck. He nudged her into the direction he wanted her to walk and the pair of them walked down the hallway and out into the night. The cold ground hurt against Robyn's bare feet as they traipsed across the car park. Her stomach turned at the thought of walking barefoot over the rodent droppings in Norman's house. Part of her wanted to fight, despite the futility, but the more distance she put between them and Wren, the better chance her sister would have.

Norman and Robyn continued down the ginnel. His vice-like grip around her hair was painful, but she would not give him the satisfaction of knowing that. Nor would she tell him how the small stones on the ground were cutting into her feet and bringing tears to her eyes. When they got to the main street, she began to veer left, but he tugged hard on her hair and pushed her to the right, in the direction of the church.

"Where are you taking me?" she said, with the knife blade now warming against her neck as the thinnest trickle of her blood coated it.

"You'll see. It's a surprise. Like the one you gave me when I was trying to be a good host, only to come out and find you were trying to leave without so much as a goodbye. That kind of surprise."

"I'm sorry. I'm sorry about that, it was wrong. It was wrong of us to do it."

"Yes. Yes it was, very wrong. But now you're going to make it up to me."

Tears began to roll down Robyn's cheeks. "Please...no," she said, her voice shaking.

"You and your sister. You're both going to make it up to me."

"No, not her. She's only fifteen. Not her," Robyn sobbed.

"Age has nothing to do with this," he said, and he guided his captive towards the pavement. "Give me your hands," he demanded. Robyn put her hands behind her and she felt something being strapped around them. She felt whatever it was tighten. "There," he said, as he nudged her back into their direction of travel. Despite the dark, Robyn could still make out the looming steeple of the church up ahead, and for the shortest time, she had a feeling that was where they were going, but suddenly, they stopped again. They had just passed a small storefront of some description. It was too dark to see what, exactly, but the large display window was a giveaway. Norman flicked on a torch. They were stood in front of a maroon coloured, wooden door which he levered open, revealing a staircase. "Move," he demanded, and Robyn began to climb the stairs.

They reached the top and there were four doors. He opened the one to the right and shone the torch inside. It was a living room, once again decorated with the most hideous, old fashioned furnishings Robyn could imagine.

He prodded her through the doorway and guided her to a sturdy wooden chair, pushing her down before proceeding to fasten her to it with the same cable ties he had used to bind her hands together.

"What are you going to do to me?" she cried.

"All in good time, Robyn. There's no rush. We've got all the time in the world now, and we wouldn't want to leave your sister out, would we?

*

The candles were flickering wildly when Wren woke up. She looked across to the window and could see from the edges of the Venetian blinds that it was still dark outside. She looked at her watch; it read four-forty a.m. There was an empty examination table next to hers; it was not there when she had gone to sleep, but she assumed that her sister had put it there. "Bobbi?" she called, but there was no response. "Bobbi?" she called, louder this time, but still there was no reply.

She peeled back the makeshift bedding that covered her and scooted across the second examination table. She carefully lowered herself to the floor. She was still a little feverish, but nothing like what she had been. As her feet touched the floor, she felt the draft more acutely from the gap underneath the door. "Bobbi," she called again. Wren grabbed the torch her sister had found with the candles and turned it on before stepping out into the corridor. "Are you having a pee?" she shouted, with a small, nervous smile. There was still no response. She began to walk down the hallway, slowly. She gently knocked on the toilet door and opened it. The various picture frames were still in place, leant carefully against the makeshift repair.

Wren moved back out into the hall, panning the torch around until she zeroed in on the front door. She went towards it and immediately felt her heart begin to race. It was slightly ajar. Her hand hovered a moment over the tarnished brass of the knob, before turning off the torch and swinging the door open, stepping out into the cold night air. She stood there on the step, looking out over the starlit car park. She turned the torch back on and shone it around like a searchlight. There was no sign of anything. "Bobbi!" she said in a whispering shout. "*Bobbi!*"

Wren went back inside and closed the door behind her. *What would have possessed her sister to go out into the night without telling her?* She walked behind the reception desk and into the small kitchen. She jumped back as the torch reflected in the window and for a split second, she thought it was someone shining a torch at her through the window. "Idiot!" she spat.

She walked back down the hallway, checking in each room as she went. "Dammit, Bobbi, where the hell are you?" Wren pulled on a pair of socks and her boots before reaching for her—her coat—it was still sat on a chair, right next to her sister's. "Shit!" the butterflies began to flap frantically in her stomach as panic set in. She grabbed her javelin, which was leant against the wall right next to Robyn's. In the unlikely event that her sister had walked out into the night, for whatever reason, there was no way she would go without her coat and without her javelin. "*Oh shiiit!*" Wren said looking underneath the examination table and seeing Robyn's boots.

Wren grabbed her sister's leather jacket and put it on. She reached into her rucksack, pulled out a Swiss Army Knife, and put it in her pocket. She took the water bottle and was about to take some more tablets when she realised she should have something to eat with them. Robyn had told her there were some open packets of biscuits in the kitchen cupboards. She headed back there, leant her javelin against a counter top, wolfed a few Garibaldis down then threw the tablets in her mouth, taking a long drink of water from her bottle. She picked her javelin up, accidentally knocking it against the mug tree on top of the microwave. The tree tipped, and Wren put out her hand to stop it, but one of the mugs fell to the ground. She waited to hear it smash, but remarkably, it remained in one piece. She picked the torch up from the counter, retrieved the mug and placed it back on the tree. She was heading out of the door again when she stopped in the entrance and went back to the mug tree. She shone her torch on one. NOR…she turned it slightly. M. And again. A. And again. N. She pulled it off the tree. NORMAN.

"Oh no!" The chances of there being two Normans in such a small village was minute. How did he work here? What could he possibly do? It didn't matter. It made sense now. He had come for her sister. He would probably come back for her too.

She opened the front door, making sure to leave it unlocked before heading out. Wren's mind raced as a blizzard of nightmarish images came towards her at full speed. Despite her better senses telling her not to, she began to jog through the car park and down the ginnel. She reached the main street and the jog became a run. Wren reached the turn that they had made earlier in the day, when they'd headed towards Norman's place. She turned the torch off, conscious of the fact it would give away her position. It took a few seconds for her eyes to adjust to the dark, but now, she could make out the outline of the hedgerow and trees along dark lane. She edged forward and put her hand out, reaching into the night until she felt the cold wrought iron of the gate underneath her fingers. She looked up the path towards the cottage. A dim light shone behind the curtains of the living room.

Wren advanced slowly up the path. The curtains were too thick to make out what was going on in the room, but she could see the flicker of real flames in the fireplace. She went to the door and pushing the handle down, opening it just a tad. The same stale air that had greeted her earlier in the day hit her again now. She fought her gag reflex and focussed, pushing the door open as quietly as she could before stepping into the dark hallway. The living room door was ajar, and the flames continued to dance among the shadows of the hallway. Wren edged down further and further, ready to confront Norman at any moment. She reached the edge of the doorway and stood there, holding the frame, dreading to see what would appear as she entered the room.

Wren took a breath and charged in, brandishing the javelin tightly in her hands. The room was empty.

She flicked on her torch and headed back out of the living room and into the kitchen, finding nothing. She went back down the hall, then began to climb the stairs carefully, stepping lightly, hoping not to hit any creaky floorboards. All the doors were already open, revealing nothing but dark, empty rooms. She walked into each to see if there was any possible clue as to where her sister might be, but there was not. Wren went to the window in the front bedroom and turned off the torch, looking out over the dark landscape of the village. "Where are you, Bobbi?" The seconds she stood there rolled into minutes as she wracked her brains trying to think where Norman could possibly have taken her sister. Then it hit her.

The first time they had seen Norman that day, he had been running up the street to warn them. Later he had told them that he had seen them from the window of his house...his other house. He might have taken her to his other place, and although she did not really know where that was, she could use her reasoning powers to try to figure it out. There were very few buildings so close to the church that would have a window in the line of sight, and the chances were, if he had taken her there, then there would be some light or candle burning. It was not as though there was anybody else left in the village. She turned around and almost ran down the stairs and back into the fresh air.

Wren kept her torch on as she jogged down the garden path, through the gate, and up the narrow lane. When she was happy she was heading back in the right direction, she flicked the torch off again, letting her eyes adjust to the dark, and continued in stealth mode, looking for the faintest flicker anywhere that might tell her where her sister was.

19

"Look, Norman, whatever you're going to do, do it to me. Wren's just a girl, leave her out of it," Robyn said as Norman was just about to head out once more.

"No. It's important she's here. I want you both here," he replied, smiling.

"You sick bastard!" she screamed.

"Quiet. You'll wake my sister," he said angrily.

"Your sister?"

"Yes. I want you and Wren to meet her."

"There are ways other than kidnapping people."

"I was going to ask you, but then you both ran out the door. All my life, people have been running away from me."

"Can't figure out why that is," Robyn replied under her breath. "Where is your sister? Does she know you're doing this?"

"My sister's not herself at the moment. She's not well."

"I'm sorry, Norman," she said, desperately trying to appeal to the side of him that was not barking mad. "What's wrong with her?"

"She's just sick."

"And what is it you think meeting me and Wren will do to help her?"

"She just needs time, that's all. She needs time to heal. I love my sister; she's the only one who has been kind to me. When no one else would give me a job, she begged the doctors at the practice, and they gave me the caretaker's job. That's a very responsible position, you know. She worked in the office there and…. My sister always helped me, always. When I got into trouble, she was always there for me. So now she needs help. Isn't it only right that I try and help her?"

"Yes. Of course. But not by hurting people, not by kidnapping them."

"I won't be long," he said, heading back out of the door.

"Norman! Norman!" she shouted, but he was gone. Robyn sat there in the candlelit room, looking around to see if she could figure out an escape. The cable ties around her wrists and ankles were tight; there was not a hope she could wriggle out of them or break free. Whatever he had planned, she had to find a way to save Wren. Then she remembered that she'd seen something in a film once where a man was tied to a chair and he toppled it over, managing to break it and get free. Robyn tensed her muscles and shifted her body weight as hard and as fast as she could to the right. The chair banged down hard, and excruciating pain shot up her arm from the elbow, but nothing broke, and the cable ties stayed in place. Now she was stuck there like a fish on the deck of a boat, floundering away, but unable to escape.

*

Wren caught sight of a torchlight heading down the street. She ducked into a doorway and stayed low as it crossed over to the other pavement. She stayed down, crouched in the shadows. The steady beam passed her and

159

she could make out Norman's silhouette as he went by and disappeared around the corner towards the doctor's surgery. Wren ran to the other side of the road and started off in the direction of the church, keeping her eyes firmly on the buildings, looking for some clue of where Norman had taken her sister. Then she saw it. A dim glow from a curtained window above one of the shops. She looked towards the steeple of the church. *Yes*, standing in that window, Norman would have been able to see them heading to the church.

Wren began to run towards the building, her head danced from side to side, trying to determine where the entrance to the upstairs flat would be. She flicked on her torch and saw a wooden door that did not belong to any of the storefronts. She tried the handle and pushed it open, leaping up the stairs, two at a time. Wren burst into the room to see her sister lying there on the floor, tied to a chair, but most definitely alive.

"Thank God!" she cried.

"Wren?"

"Don't worry, I'll cut you free," Wren said, putting down her javelin and pulling out her penknife.

"Hurry, he won't be long."

"I know," she said, cutting through the cable ties one at a time. She sliced through the last one, and Robyn jumped to her feet. The two sisters embraced tightly then both headed for the door. "I saw him going to the—" The living room door slammed shut and a key turned in the lock.

"What the f—"

"At least I've got you both here now," Norman shouted through the door. "It won't be long, then you can meet my sister."

"Let us out...now!" demanded Wren, banging on the dirty paint of the door.

"Soon. Soon," he said.

The girls heard another door unlock and creak open. "Who has locks on internal doors?" Wren asked.

"It's not that uncommon in older places; you won't remember Gran's house. But actually using them...that's something else," Robyn replied.

Wren took a tight hold of her javelin and aimed it towards the door, ready to strike. In the absence of anything else that could be used as a weapon, Robyn picked up an old looking vase and held it ready to throw. They heard the door unlock and held their breaths, expecting Norman to come bursting in, but instead, the door stayed closed.

Wren and Robyn looked towards each other, but remained in battle pose, ready to strike. After a full minute, when the door had still not opened, Robyn went towards it. "Okay," she whispered, "I'll swing it open. If he's there, stick him."

"What?"

"Stab him with the javelin."

"But...I...he's a human being."

"Yeah, a human being who was about to do god knows what to you and me." Robyn marched towards her sister and took the javelin from her, handing her the vase instead. "Go open the door."

Wren stood behind the door for a moment, psyching herself up before flinging it open, revealing...nothing, other than a very small, very empty landing. She turned on her torch and looked back towards her sister.

"Run. Now!" Robyn said, and Wren began to thunder down the stairs. Robyn took hold of the bannister with one hand, kept the javelin in the other, and backed down the stairs, slowly, ready for Norman to leap out of the darkness towards her.

"It's locked!" cried Wren as she desperately tried to open the door. "There's no key."

"Out of the way," Robyn said, trying the doorknob herself. "Crap! Okay. We'll look for another way out. God knows where he's gone I've no doubt he'll be back soon."

The two sisters started heading back up the stairs when a sound made them freeze, in more ways than one. Wren shone the torch up to the landing, and there, stood at the top was Norman, holding a woman in an old-fashioned pink, flowery summer dress. Her hands were bound in front of her, and her grey-brown curly locks fell over her shoulders from beneath the cloth bag that covered her head.

Wren and Robyn stood in silence, neither able to breathe, both dreading what Norman would do next with the poor soul he had bound at the top of the stairs. Finally, he made his move, pulling the bag from over the woman's head and taking off the gag, all while keeping a tight hold on the dog collar he had around her neck. A growl started at the back of the woman's throat, and Wren panned the torch beam to her face. The familiar grey eyes of a creature glared back at her, the pupils nearly taking up the whole of the eyes in the darkness of the stairwell.

It tugged against the restraints of the cable tie at the sight of fresh prey, almost oblivious to the fact it was being held in place. It struggled and writhed, trying to reach the two girls, but couldn't. Then Norman released it. And the beast flew, literally, as it lost its footing at the top of the stairs due to its raging hunger. It cartwheeled in the torch spotlight and there was a stomach-churning crack as a bone broke, echoing up and down the stairwell, "*Nooo!*" cried Norman, charging down the stairs after it.

The two girls jumped to either side as the tumbling creature landed hard against the front door with another deafening thud. Wren's hand shook, but the rest of her was paralyzed with fear. When they were both stuck in the living room, Robyn had been ready to do what she needed to, to protect her sister. But now, she too was numbed at the horrific sight, as the creature lay battered against the door, its neck nearly at a right angle to its shoulders. Its hands were still bound together in front, almost as if it was praying, which, subconsciously, the girls were doing at that very moment.

"Lizzie…. No, Lizzie," cried Norman as he reached the bottom of the stairs. Robyn suddenly raised the javelin, ready to stab if he made a move towards either her or Wren, but now his madness had a different focus as he knelt down and clutched the broken figure. "No!" he said again with tears beginning to roll down his face. Let's get you back upstairs. A good night's rest and you'll be as right as rain."

"Stop!" shouted, Robyn. "Let us out! Let us out of here."

Norman stopped in his tracks. He looked towards Robyn in the torchlight. The tears glistened in his eyes. He held his sister close to him with one hand, while reaching into his pocket and pulling out the keys. Robyn stepped over to Wren's side as he unlocked and opened the door. "A good night's sleep that's all you need," he said again.

The two girls backed out of the doorway. Robyn kept the javelin raised, ready to strike if Norman made a move, but his insane grief had consumed him, taking his entire focus. Wren kept the torchlight on him, just in case.

The door closed, and the two girls stood there, in a state of shock.

"What the hell just happened?" Wren asked.

"That was his sister, I think," Robyn replied.

"His sister?"

"When he had me tied up there, he kept talking about how he wanted you and me to meet his sister."

"He was completely crazy. Did you see the look in his eyes?"

"I don't want to think about it."

Wren looked around her. It was beginning to get light. "Well, that felt like the longest night of my life."

Robyn looked up to the sky, then back towards her sister. "How are you feeling?"

"Oh, I feel great. Having a brilliant time."

"No, I mean, how's your wound?"

Wren placed her hand on it gently. "It doesn't feel too bad. A lot better than it did." Wren looked down at Robyn's bare feet. "How are your feet?"

"Agony. Cut to ribbons. But we can sort them out when we get back to the surgery. Then, I think we need to get out of here. Do you feel up to getting back on the road? I promise, the next time we stop, it will be for longer, but we need to get the hell away from psycho-boy while he's preoccupied with his sister."

They began walking back slowly in the direction of the surgery. "Would you have killed him, Bobbi?"

"He abducted me and held a knife to my throat, tied me up and went for my little sister. He was going to feed us to zombie Lizzie, for god's sake, Wren."

"You're right, it's just…. Killing someone. That's different to killing these things."

"All that matters is you and me. I'll do whatever it takes to keep us safe...to keep us alive."

"Muuummm!" shouted Norman, bursting back out of his door. "Something's wrong with Lizzie, very wrong," he cried, running up the street towards the church. "Muuummm! You've got to help."

"What the hell?" Robyn said as she and Wren turned around to watch Norman speed waddle up the street.

"I thought he said his mum was dead," Wren said.

"He did, he said she was…oh no. Even he couldn't be that insane, surely?"

Robyn and Wren stood there in the middle of the street as they watched Norman. He opened the gate to the churchyard and bounded up the path. "Muuummm!" he cried again before pulling open the church doors. It was like watching a horror film that they'd seen before. They knew what was going to happen, but they were scared stiff anyway. In less than a minute, Norman was no longer visible, although his screams of agony echoed around the village. In the early morning light, all Wren and Robyn could see was a throng of movement at the entrance of the church. The creatures were free, all of them, and now, more than ever, the two sisters needed to escape this hellish place once and for all.

They moved over to the pavement and kept low, looking back constantly to see if they had been spotted by the beasts. They finally reached the footpath that led to the surgery and ducked down it, moving as fast as they could. They climbed the surgery steps, opened the door and dived in, locking the door quietly behind them.

They headed straight for the room they had bedded down in for the night. "We need to get your feet sorted, otherwise we won't make it a hundred yards," Wren said. "Get on the table."

Robyn did not argue, and climbed onto the examination table. Wren placed a torch down, giving her sufficient light to work with. "Are they bad?"

"Compared to what?" Wren replied.

"Stop kidding around."

"They're badly cut in places, Bobbi. I'm going to have to clean them and bandage them."

"Please be quick."

Wren grabbed a big wad of cotton wool from a jar and the bottle of alcohol that Robyn had used on her the day before. She poured the alcohol over the cotton wool. "Take a breath," she said, as she dabbed the wadded wool against her sister's wounds.

Robyn's fist shot up to her mouth and she bit down on it to avoid screaming at the pain. Her feet were still bleeding, but there was nothing particularly deep. Wren pulled out the antiseptic cream from her rucksack and squeezed a good dollop from the tube onto her fingers before placing it onto her sister's feet. "Gross," she said.

"What's gross?" Robyn asked.

"Your feet. They're like pig's trotters."

"Cow!"

"No, pig." The two girls tried to smile, but it did not work. They knew how dire their situation was. They were both injured. They were both in pain. They had endured the most horrifying night of their life, and the day ahead did not look like it was going to be an improvement.

Wren pulled out two bandages and two safety pins from her rucksack. She tore the first packet open and carefully began to wrap the cloth around her sister's left foot, before securing it into place.

"You're really good at that," Robyn said.

"I had to dress plenty of my own wounds and sprains," she said, moving straight on to the next one. She finished the second dressing and delved into her sister's rucksack for some socks. Wren caringly placed them over Robyn's bandages. "How does that feel?"

"Good."

"Good," Wren replied. "It's a shame; if we had time there are so many supplies we could take from here."

"We'll find other places, we'll find other supplies. Right now, we need to get out of here as fast as we can," Robyn replied, pulling on her boots.

"You're right. Just a shame, that's all."

Robyn climbed down from the examination table, and Wren suddenly realised she was still wearing her sister's jacket. She started to unzip it, but Robyn stopped her. "It looks better on you anyway," she said, pulling a thick cotton shirt out of her bag and rolling up the sleeves. She put on her rucksack, picked up the javelin and the holdall and the two of them headed to the door.

Wren turned off the torch. It was not particularly bright out yet, but it was light enough for them to see, and they did not want to attract attention in case any of the creatures were lurking. Almost sensing what her sister was thinking, Wren said, "Let's hope they're still up at the far end of the street."

They reached the front door and both of them looked at each other before pushing it open. They stood on the step for a few seconds, then headed down, across the car park and to the narrow alleyway that led out onto the main street. They walked slowly, Wren in front, as she was able to keep both her hands on the javelin. As they reached the end, they stopped and crouched down. Wren looked down the street first. That would be their direction of travel. It was clear. She swapped sides and looked up towards the church. The feast was over and the beasts had begun to spread out. There were still a number of them in the church grounds, but others had meandered, scouring their surroundings for fresh prey.

She let out a small gasp as she spotted Norman. His grey tank top was now dyed purple with blood from his neck and shoulder wounds. His overweight corpse waddled with little purpose, but he and another beast were only a few metres up the street, and there was no way the sisters could make a break for it without being seen.

Wren turned to Robyn, "We've got a big problem."

20

Robyn and Wren sat on the examination table. The Venetian blinds were closed. They had locked the front door and made sure all the downstairs windows at least were covered one way or another.

"This is my fault," Robyn said. "We should have just gone. If you hadn't bandaged my feet, we'd have been out of here while they were all still snacking on Nutjob Norman."

"Don't be stupid. You wouldn't have got to the end of the street with your feet the way they are."

"So, what now?"

"So now we need a plan."

"Great. All our plans have worked out so well."

"Okay, so, right this minute, we're safe. Those things don't know we're here. They can't see inside; we're not in danger—provided we don't venture outside."

"And?"

"Well, we need to decide. Are we going to stay here, while we get better, while my wound heals, while your feet heal, or are we going to go?"

"Are you honestly suggesting we stay here?"

"It's not as stupid as it sounds."

"Explain it to me, because staying in a village full of flesh-eating zombies sounds pretty stupid to me."

"Right, listen, we take a couple of days. My wound feels a lot better than it did, but I'm still not one hundred per cent. Your feet aren't great. A couple of days' care and they'll be a lot better. We've got food. We've got water. I don't know how long our gas canister will last, but we can have hot food while it does. And during this time, we can strip this place of supplies and come up with an idea of how the hell we're going to get out of here unseen, which right this minute, I have no clue about."

Robyn turned to look at Wren, her brow was creased. "I don't want to stay here. I want to get out."

"Okay, whatever decision we make, it will be a joint one. How are we going to get out?"

"I...I don't know."

"Well, until we have a plan, we're not going anywhere, so maybe we should just rest for a little while. It's been a long night."

"We're trapped here, aren't we? We're going to die in this village," Robyn said.

"You're tired and you're in pain. When you feel better, you'll see things in a different light."

"How can you stay so positive?"

"What else is there, Bobbi? Every time I lost a race, a throw, a jump, an event...every time I got an injury...if I gave in to my doubts, if I gave in to that little nagging voice in my head, that would have been it. I'd have packed up my kit, gone home and probably taken up stamp collecting or something. But god bless my old twisted perv of a coach, because he told me how to get stuff done. He told me how to fight back."

"I wish he was here now, maybe he could show me."

"You don't need him, you've got me. We're going to get out of this. I know it looks impossible. It looks like we're stuck here, but we're not."

"Oh really?"

"We can head out of that front door now and make a run for it."

"And what do you think our chances would be, exactly?"

"Pretty bad."

Robyn slipped her boots off and lay down on the examination table, closing her eyes. "You're so awesome at motivational speeches, Wren. I feel much better now. That coach taught you well. Oh god, please kill me now," she said looking up at the ceiling.

Wren jumped down from the table and turned to look at her sister. "You asked me what I thought our chances were if we headed out there now and I told you. That's because I'm injured, you're injured, and we don't have a plan. That doesn't mean that we couldn't do it; we still have that choice. I just don't think it would be a good idea." The words slowly computed in Robyn's brain. She opened her eyes and turned to look towards her sister. "Now, if you just asked me what I thought our chances in general were, I would say, brilliant. Look at what we've done in the past couple of days. Look at how far we've come. What we're capable of that we didn't think we ever could be before. God, Bobbi! You were going to kill a man to protect us. You and I have been working together as a team. I never thought I'd see the day, but we've worked together well, and when we've put our minds to something, we've done it."

"So, what are you saying?"

"I'm saying if you and I rest up. If we get match fit, then we can get out of this place. And I'm not just saying this stuff to make you feel better—I know we can do it."

"Okay. Say we do it your way. How long do we stay here?"

"Two days, three tops. We heal, we eat, we prepare supplies and we form a plan. Then when we're ready, we go, we head out, and we find the place we want to stay. The place that we're going to call home from now on. Somewhere that's safe."

Robyn leant up on her elbow. "Okay...maybe you're a bit better at motivational speeches than I gave you credit for. We'll do it your way. We'll rest up, then we'll make a break for it, but I've got some conditions."

"Go on."

"Absolutely no torches, no lights on after dark. I don't want any of those things knowing we're in here."

"Agreed."

"We don't go outside at all until we're ready to go."

"Agreed."

"We condense our supplies to just the two rucksacks."

"Agreed."

"And I get the last of the Garibaldi biscuits."

"You drive a hard bargain," Wren said, smiling.

"Now that's been decided, we should probably get some sleep. I'm pretty certain I didn't get my full eight hours last night," Robyn said turning over onto her side.

"I'll join you in a little while, I'm just going to go have a snoop around the place. I wasn't really up to it yesterday."

"Okay. But don't wake me when you come back in."

"Scooch over to the other side, then I won't have to." Robyn tutted, but then shuffled across to the other examination table and settled down to sleep.

Even with all the downstairs windows covered, there was enough light for Wren to see. She headed up the stairs, and even though she could feel her wound pulling a little, it was nowhere near as bad as it had been. She walked into the supply room where she had found her sister, and her eyes lit up. There were shelving units full of everything from tablets and medicines to bandages and

171

medicinal alcohol. She picked up one of the bottles and saw the flammable sign on the side of it, and her lips curled into a smile. She would definitely have to stock up before they left this place, there was way too much good stuff to leave behind.

She walked into the office lined with filing cabinets, making sure she avoided walking past the windows just in case there were any creatures looking in her direction. Wren sat down at the desk and opened the top drawer; there was nothing of any interest. She moved down to the deeper drawer at the bottom to find boxes of pens, a spare stapler, staples. She pulled it out farther and saw the top of a red cap. She grabbed hold of it; it was a small bottle of vodka.

"Result!" she said. "I suppose the life of a filing clerk can get a little dull from time to time." She examined the drawer further to find out if there was anything thing else exciting, but there wasn't. Wren headed back downstairs with a smile on her face. She had been drunk once in her life, on champagne when they'd found out she'd been chosen for the Commonwealth Games squad. She didn't like the after effects, but she remembered feeling very relaxed at the time. A little stress relief for her and her sister might not be a bad thing now.

She went back downstairs and into the kitchen. She was not hungry but ate a couple of biscuits so she could take her tablets before heading back into their room. Robyn was sound asleep, and Wren climbed onto the examination table next to her, curled up, and drifted off.

*

It was mid-afternoon when a scream jolted Wren from her dreams. Her eyes shot open and she tried desperately to get her bearings. Her sister was still curled up on the other examination table, but an eerie high-pitched sound was coming from her direction. Wren shuffled up onto one elbow and reached across, placing a hand on Robyn's arm and rubbing it up and down, gently. "Bobbi. It's okay, Bobbi, it's okay. You're just having a nightmare." The sound continued to rise, so Wren took a firm hold of her sister's arm and shook it. "Bobbi...Bobbi..."

"Mum!" screamed Robyn, waking herself up. She flipped around like she was still stuck in her nightmare, and Wren withdrew her hand. Robyn's eyes were wide, her breathing was erratic. She looked at her sister, but for a few seconds, it was almost as if she did not recognise her.

"Bobbi, you were having a nightmare."

Robyn blinked and looked around the room, taking everything in. Her breathing was still erratic, but her eyes started to look a little more normal as the seconds ticked by. "It was...horrible."

"It's okay," Wren said, reaching out to put a reassuring hand on her once again.

"You, me, and Dad were sat at the dinner table, then Mum brought our plates across. It was sweet n' sour chicken. Dad told us about his day, as usual, Mum told us about hers. They asked about our days at school and then when dinner was over, we all just sat there with our empty plates in front of us. Mum and Dad just had these smiles on their faces, looking at us both. It got really weird because no matter what we said to them, they wouldn't answer. They just kept looking at us with these smiles. Then their faces started changing. The colour drained out of them, they started turning grey, and then their eyes clouded over. They stayed in their chairs, just looking at us. We panicked; we were shouting and screaming, but we didn't pull back from the table, it was like we were glued there..."

"Then what happened?"

"Then the smiles disappeared and their mouths opened a little. The growling started, and you and I were screaming and crying and we reached across to hold each other's hands. We were begging them to stop as if they had some power over what was happening, but the growls got louder and louder. Then Dad dived at you with his arms outstretched and Mum dived towards me. That's when I woke up."

"Note to self: Never sleep again. I'm not surprised you screamed. That's horrible...I feel scared just hearing it."

"Thank you for waking me."

"You've woken me from enough nightmares in the past. Remember after we watched the first Paranormal Activity film?" Wren said, trying to lighten the mood.

Robyn allowed herself to succumb to the memory. "Oh my god. It was like a full week after that, that you were still sneaking into my bed when I was asleep."

"And who was to blame for that?"

"What do you mean? You made me watch the sequel, then you waited until I'd gone to sleep and came to stand by my bed in a white sheet."

Robyn burst out laughing. "I'd forgotten."

"How could you forget that? Mum grounded you for like, ten years."

"Dad thought it was funny," Robyn said, laughing.

"He did until I woke the house up every night with my screaming, and him and Mum both had to go to work." The two sisters laughed again.

"That's right..." Robyn shook her head.

"Hey, look what I found," Wren said, climbing from the examination table and walking over to the desk. She proudly picked up the bottle of vodka. "I thought we could have it tonight."

"Erm, that's not a good idea."

"Why?" Wren asked, looking hurt.

"For a start, you're on antibiotics, painkillers and anti-inflammatories. Secondly, I think we're going to need our wits about us. If something happens and we're both pished, it's not going to end well."

Wren put the bottle down on the table, and her head sunk. "I suppose you're right. I just…"

"Just what?"

"It doesn't matter."

"No, tell me," Robyn said, sliding from the examination table.

"It's just…this is the closest I've felt to you in years. I feel like after all this time, we're really bonding, not just as sisters, but friends as well. I thought it would be fun to get drunk together."

Robyn walked across and picked up the bottle of vodka, placing it in her rucksack. "Look, I promise, when we get to our next place, we'll open it up. We'll have a girl's night. We don't need to get drunk to bond." She walked back and sat down on the edge of the exam table. "It's my fault, Wren. I was so wrapped up in my friends and going out and having a good time that I neglected you. We used to be close growing up, then when you started with the training, we drifted."

"I didn't want it like that. I thought you might have been proud when I started doing well. I thought, maybe you'd come and see me at one of the competitions."

"Like I said, Wren, it's on me. I should have been more supportive. I shut myself away in my own selfish world without realising just how amazing you'd become."

"I'm hardly amazing."

"You don't see it, but I do. You saved us. If it hadn't been for you, I wouldn't be breathing now. I don't know many fifteen-year-old girls who can do what you do." Wren's cheeks suddenly flushed red. "Trust me. I'm sorry for not being there, but things will be different from now on." The two sisters smiled each other.

"I can't believe you gave up your mobile phone for us."

"Yeah well, I figured it was more important to think about the family I still had than the family I'd lost."

Robyn's face warmed again into the most affectionate of smiles. "Now what is there to eat? I'm starving."

21

The two sisters spent the rest of the day, and the day after that, doing very little other than talking and resting. Very occasionally, one of them would venture up to the second floor and carefully position themselves at the side of the window in the office to see if any of the monsters had strayed into the car park, but none had. From the creatures they had dealt with so far, there were no lingering remnants of the people they had been. They had seen that with their own father. Whatever these things were, they were left with nothing but primal instinct. They did not have to worry about Norman seeking them out. Norman was gone. The whole village was gone. As far as Wren and Robyn were concerned, the whole world might be gone by now.

On the third day, Wren and Robyn woke up rested. They had spent a full night with uninterrupted sleep. Wren's wound, although still evident, was no longer hurting; it was a healthy colour, and she could bend and walk up and down the stairs without putting undue pressure on it. Likewise, Robyn could stand and walk around without too much discomfort.

Wren headed to the toilet to get washed, while Robyn went into the kitchen. They turned on the hot water tap and started washing themselves, and at virtually the same time they called out to each other: "The water's gone off."

Robyn walked into the hallway in just her bra and knickers. Wren came out of the toilet in a t-shirt with soap all over her face. "I suppose that's the hot water tank used up," Wren said, wiping the white sheen off with a towel.

"I'm going to sue under trade descriptions. There hasn't been hot water for days."

"You realise, that means the only water we've got left is what's in our rucksacks now. That means—"

"I know what it means," interrupted Robyn. "So how soon do we need to go?

"We've got enough for today and tomorrow," Wren replied.

"So?"

"So!"

"You want to set off today?"

"I don't think we can risk leaving it any longer," Wren replied.

"We don't even have a plan."

"Well, I've been thinking about that."

"And?"

"Okay, this is a pretty big building."

"And?"

"Well, I'd say there were no more than forty of those things, maybe forty-five at a push."

"And?"

"I could lead them through the front door, and we could make our escape out of the back."

"That's your idea? And people call you the smart one," Robyn said.

"No, listen, I've simplified it. We set up a barricade, here," Wren said, pointing to the area just before the room where they had been staying. I lead them in through the front door. I vault the barrier, then you and I head out of the back, and we're on our way.

"And how do you propose to just 'vault the barrier?' I know high jump's one of your events, sis, but I don't see any big bendy poles around here, do you?"

"Look, we'll figure that part out in a minute, but in essence, that's the plan. It'll work, Bobbi, I know it will."

"That sounds like a really, really bad plan. I don't like the idea of you going out there and those things chasing you. So much can go wrong."

"Okay, what are our options?"

Robyn just looked at her. She didn't have any better ideas and she knew it. She let out a long resigned breath. "Alright, you win. We'll do it your way."

"Let's finish getting dressed, and then we'll get to work."

Within a few minutes, the girls were stood back in the hallway, fully dressed. "So, this is your show; tell me what you want me to do," Robyn said.

"Okay, this might sound a little crazy, but trust me, it's not."

"Those are words that always fill me with confidence. Go on."

"We build in layers to the barricade, because when there are loads of those things, there's going to be quite a lot of weight. Even though we're only talking a few seconds before we disappear out the back, it might be the difference between us getting out and us not."

"Okay, I'm listening."

"Okay," Wren said, walking down the hall and building the image with her hands. "We have two rows of filing cabinets, here, filled with files and whatever crap we can find to weigh them down. We place them facing away, so there is no danger of a drawer opening and those things being able to clamber over. And here, we have two of the large desks; we make sure they're weighted down too."

"And how exactly are you going to get over? Those filing cabinets come up to our necks; it's not like you can just step onto them," Robyn said.

"Yeah, well that's the tricky part."

"Oh, there's a tricky part? That's good, it was all sounding way too easy."

"We put one of the smaller cabinets, and another of the taller filing cabinets further down the hall. I'll come in running through the door; leap onto the small cabinet, springboard off that onto the taller cabinet, then a long jump, onto the top of the other filing cabinets here, down onto the desk and onto the floor. Voila. We can't have the smaller cabinet and the other filing cabinet too close, cos there's always the risk they could topple and those things might be able to climb over."

"Oh my god! You're as mad as Norman. That's crazy. You're going to kill yourself trying something like that," Robyn said, outraged.

"Bobbi, long jump is one of my best events. I've done this a thousand times, over much longer distances."

"You're right, sorry, I shouldn't doubt you. I'm forgetting the 2012 games when I saw Jessica Ennis take her run-up, leap onto a small filing cabinet then onto a taller one, finally coming to land on another set of filing cabinets, and finishing her slide on a wooden desk, all while being chased by forty zombies. I thought to myself back then, 'Oh. That looks like a piece of piss. Why are they handing medals out for this crap?' You're mental. MENTAL. You will end up dead if you try that."

"Trust me, I know I can do this. If it makes you feel any better, we can take the pads and cushions of the examination table to soften the landing."

"Yeah, that would make me feel a lot better, 'cos it was the landing I was worried about. Everything seemed straightforward up to that point."

Wren grabbed hold of her sister's hand. "I *can* do this. Now come on, let's get to work," she said, smiling.

It took them over ninety minutes to build the barricade. All the cabinets needed emptying due to the weight before they could be moved. Then the two sisters refilled them with their original contents, and more besides, making sure they were rock solid. They laid it out exactly as Wren had suggested. Wren climbed onto the desk and stood on top of the cabinets, springing up and down on them a few times. "See, solid as anything," she said, climbing down and heading across to the freestanding set of drawers farther down the hallway. She pushed hard against it, but it barely moved. They had not only filled them with the files but with reams of paper, scales from the examination rooms, gallon containers of disinfectant from the cleaning cupboard, anything they could find. She walked over to the smaller cabinet; she tried to push it, but it felt glued into position.

"I want to see you do it," Robyn said, climbing onto the desk so she could see her sister beyond the barricade. "I want to see you make the jump."

"I can't. There's not enough room. When I come in, I'll be going at full pelt; I'll already have momentum. I can't go from standing still to doing the jump."

"I really don't like this. I don't like this at all."

"It is what it is, Bobbi. It will be fine."

"If anything happens to you, Wren, I'll…"

Wren walked back towards her sister. "You'll what?"

"I'll never forgive myself. It should be me heading out there, not you. It should be me taking the risks."

"Bobbi. I can do the two hundred in twenty-five flat. I can jump six metres; this is only half that distance," she said, pointing back to the filing cabinet. "It will be fine. Trust me." Wren placed her hands on top of the filing cabinets and pulled herself up. Robyn offered a hand and helped her to her feet. The two sisters looked down the hall and into the foyer, visualising how it was all going to unfold, before climbing down onto the desks, then to the floor. They went back into their room and without saying a word, prepared their rucksacks. As requested, Wren had thinned out the contents so they would no longer be carrying the holdall around too.

They fastened each of them and carried them out to the rear of the hall, placing them by the back door, ready for a quick escape.

"Right then. This is it, I suppose," Wren said.

Robyn threw her arms around her sister. "Promise me you'll be careful. I don't want to face this alone. I want it to be you and me."

"Just be ready to run like hell when I get back." She was just about to head out, then she stopped. "Oh man, nearly forgot one of the most important pieces of the puzzle."

"What?"

"Won't be a minute," Wren said climbing back over the barricade. She returned a moment later with a glass bottle that once contained lemonade, and walked back into their room. Robyn followed her and watched as she filled the bottle with surgical alcohol before stuffing some cotton wool in the top. She checked that the lighter was still in her pocket, and the straight-edged screwdriver was tucked into her belt. "Okay. Time to have some fun," she said, heading out and opening the back door.

Robyn handed her the javelin. "Don't forget this," she said.

"I can't take that, Bobbi."

"What do you mean? Why?"

"I won't be able to make the jump with the javelin. I've got the screwdriver if I run into trouble."

"Oh god! This just gets worse and worse," Robyn said.

"Just don't worry."

Wren climbed back onto the desk, onto the top of the filing cabinets, and sat down before sliding off the edge onto the other side. She walked down the hall and into the foyer. She looked at the staircase and up to the tall ceiling. "It's a shame. This would have been a beautiful house once. We could have settled here, if it wasn't for those things."

"We'll find somewhere better."

Wren smiled. "Yeah," she said, looking out of the side window to make sure the car park was clear. When she determined it was, she opened the front door and placed a wedge underneath it to make sure it did not swing shut. "Smell you later," she said, forcing a smile.

"Yeah. Smell ya later, sis."

22

Despite the car park being clear, Wren instinctively stayed quiet and low as she ran across, holding the bottle firmly in her right hand. She leapfrogged the small verge of bushes that separated the car park from the pavement and headed down the narrow alley towards the main street. As she reached the end, she stopped and crouched down lower, pressing her back hard against the wall to the right, and edging out as far as she could without being seen. The route out of the village was all clear. She let out a sigh. Maybe she was overthinking this. Maybe she and Robyn could just slip out without any theatrics.

She moved over to the other side of the alleyway and did the same thing. A breath caught in her throat as she saw one of the creatures with its back to her, not more than ten metres away. Others were meandering around, sniffing at the air, trying to pick up the scent of prey. She shuffled back a little, knowing that if the thing turned around, it would see her. She moved a little further down the alley and pulled the lighter from her pocket.

The flame made the cotton wool wick smoulder for a moment before it began to burn. Wren knew she could not afford the luxury of just throwing the homemade incendiary device across the street; she would be too easy to spot. She wanted to be spotted, but only when the time was right. She edged back down to the end of the ginnel, took a deep breath and launched the bottle as high as she could into the air, leaving all the creatures in the near vicinity oblivious to its origin. She was only a few centimetres back from the main street as she watched the bottle arc diagonally across the street. It smashed on the roof of a building three units up. Flames dripped over the side, and burning alcohol collected in the plastic guttering.

The sun was shining and the effect of the flames was a little camouflaged by its brightness, but within a few seconds, black smoke began to rise into the air. The sound alone had attracted all the creatures within earshot, and their growling chorus rose in excitement. They did not understand how the flames started. They did not understand what the flames were, but their animal instinct told them it was not something they could produce. It was something alien.

They stood looking up at the roof as the fire caught a greater hold. Wren pulled back from the edge of the alley and headed back into the car park, nestling behind some bushes. The first part of the plan had been executed. The fire was taking hold. Now she just had to wait a few minutes until it really caught, and every single one of the creatures in the village had assembled to see it. Then it was time for phase two.

Wren remained crouched for a few more minutes, but as the loud crackle of the flames began to drown out the creatures' growls, she stood up. It was nearly time. She began to loosen up, bending and stretching, making sure nothing twanged when she needed to rely on her body for the most important race of her life. When she was content that she was as limber as she could get, she headed back down the ginnel. Wren looked up to the sky and saw that it was filling with dark grey smoke. "God, I hope this works."

She reached the end of the alley and stepped out onto the main street. The roof of the building was fully ablaze and the fire had spread to the one next door. The guttering was melting, sending acrid black smoke into the afternoon air. Wren looked at the creatures; they were transfixed by the display, searching between the flames and the smoke for any sign of something edible.

Wren took another step out into the street. The nearest beast was just ten feet away with its back to her.

All the cocksureness and bravado she had displayed to her sister suddenly left her and she felt her legs start shaking. She ducked back into the ginnel. *Oh God, she thought, I'm not going to be able to go through with it.* Her breathing got faster and her nostrils began to coat with the residue of the smoke. If she was going to do this, she would need to do it now. If she started coughing and spluttering, it was all over.

Wren stood up straight and took a deep breath while she still could. She stepped out into the street once more.

"*Aaarrrggghhh!*" she screamed at the top of her voice. As if they were a flock of birds, all the creatures turned their heads and started towards her in one fluid movement. The sheer scale and speed of the advance took Wren by surprise and she lost a valuable second as her body tried to catch up with her mind. She turned and started running as fast as she could. Just in those first few metres, her ears could no longer hear the fire. Everything was drowned out by the sound of thundering feet and excited growls. As she sprinted down the alleyway, she could hear the creatures pounding behind her, she could hear their terrifying chorus, she could hear them jostling for position. Then as she leapt over the dividing verge she heard some of them trip over the bushes and go sprawling on the tarmac, but she could not allow herself the luxury of a glance. This race would come down to the wire and the hardest stretch was still ahead.

Wren powered across the car park, certain that she was making better time than she ever had on the track. She leapt up the three wide steps leading to the entrance and hurtled through the door, seeing the waiting room chair standing there, looking so flimsy now it was time to put her plan into action. As the first creatures followed her in, barging through the doorway, the growls filled the foyer and hall. In the confines of the building, everything became a lot more real. The next few seconds would be the difference between life and death.

Wren could almost feel the outstretched fingers of the predators grasping the air behind her as she ran. Timing, positioning, strength, balance—they all counted now, more than ever. She launched, and her breathing paused. Wren's left foot landed firmly on the smaller cabinet; in that microsecond, she felt the top of it give a little under her weight, but it did not crumble and she pushed off harder, flying even higher now. Her right foot hit the top of the cabinet in the middle of the hallway hard, and now she put every grain of her strength into the final part of the jump. Her eyes focussed on the gap between the two tall metal cabinets, then beyond them to Robyn. She had never seen her sister look so fretful, so scared; not even when they were little girls. But now, as Wren soared higher still like she had indeed sprouted wings, she looked down at Robyn and she saw not her older sister, but the girl from their childhood. Wren's arms swung and waved, making sure she kept steady, making sure she kept on course. She brought her feet down on top of one of the filing cabinets with a deafening metallic clunk; she felt the metal cave a little with the sheer force. This was not like jumping into a sandpit. She extended her right leg as her body jolted forward with the momentum; her foot banged down on the solid wooden desk, slowing her a little further, and sending a shock through her whole body.

"*Argh!*" she grunted, but was unable to come to a stop. Then she saw her sister had laid the pads and cushions from the examination tables in front of the desk, anticipating this very problem. Wren brought both her feet up as she aimed for a soft landing on the double thickness of the pads. Her heels dug into the top layer and even though it slipped off the bottom one, the speed and force had dissipated substantially. Wren slid across the carpet on the pad for a few feet as the creatures smashed into the barrier with an almighty crunch.

She swung round to see arms still desperately grasping and grabbing the air in front of them, but with no chance of reaching either her or her sister. Robyn offered her hand to Wren, who took it as she climbed to her feet.

"I love you," Robyn said.

"You don't have to constantly say it y'know," she said as the two of them hugged tightly.

"Smart arse."

The noise got louder as the rest of the creatures crowded into the foyer and down the hall in a desperate attempt to reach the two girls. "I'm big on hugs, but I think we'd better make tracks, don't you?"

The two girls remained in their embrace as they looked at the horde of malevolent beasts reaching out towards them.

"Probably a good call."

Wren and Robyn headed to the back door, picked up their rucksacks and javelins, took one last look in the direction of the barricade, and left.

They shut the door behind them, then scurried around the front of the building. Wren peeked around the corner, but there was no sign of anything. If creatures had indeed fallen, as she had suspected, they had gathered themselves and followed their brethren into the building in search of fresh flesh.

Wren crept up to the front door and looked around the corner. All the beasts were still desperate to break through the barricade, sure that wherever the two girls had fled, they could still reach them. Wren quietly closed the door until she heard that latch slide into place. "Let's get the hell out of here."

They jogged across the car park, vaulted the small verge, ran down the alley, and paused for a moment to see the spectacle unfolding across the street. The fire had taken hold of more of the rooftops and spread to the upper floors of one of the units.

"Is that your handy work?" Robyn asked.

"It got the job done."

"So basically, you burnt down the whole village to make sure we could escape?"

"Like I say, it got the job done."

The black smoke billowed and the fire showed no sign of slowing down. "C'mon, we've got some ground to cover before we can rest again."

The pair of them began to jog down the street, leaving the burning buildings behind them. They reached the turn for Norman's house but carried straight on. It was a country lane, surrounded by hedges and trees. Farmer's fields sat on either side and within a few minutes, the air was fresh, the sun was shining, and the hellish inferno was behind them. They remained quiet as they put distance between themselves and the catastrophe. After several minutes they slowed down to take a breath and looked back to the direction they'd come from. Thick black smoke continued to spiral into the sky.

"We should climb over the fence. It doesn't make sense to be on the road," Wren said.

"Why? They're trapped in the surgery, they can't come after us."

"I'm not thinking about them. If there are any others in sight of that smoke, they're going to be heading towards it."

"Oh god—I didn't even think of that. Real little Miss Sunshine you are."

Wren and Robyn carried on walking until they reached a large gate. They climbed over and moved across to the wall on the opposite side of the field before carrying on their journey.

After an hour, when the heat of the sun became too much for them to walk in, they sat down under a tree and ate. There was very little gas left in the small camp stove, so they decided to save that for an evening meal. Wren tugged at the ring pull on a tin of spaghetti hoops and offered it to her sister.

"Yum, cold spaghetti," she said.

"Better than cold nothing," Wren replied, grabbing a bottle from her rucksack and taking a long drink of water.

"I suppose," Robyn replied, digging her fork into the orange sauce.

"I hope we find somewhere soon," Wren said.

"What's the matter? We've still got plenty of daylight left."

Wren lifted up her t-shirt to reveal her wound had opened up again. "I think it will be okay, but I could feel that last jump really pulled on it."

Robyn's shoulders sagged, and she handed the tin of spaghetti to Wren. "I suppose that was only to be expected under the circumstances."

"Okay, we'll finish lunch and set off again, straight away."

They sat, ate, and drank for fifteen minutes before getting to their feet again. The sun got hotter and they took t-shirts out of their rucksacks, fashioning makeshift headscarves out of them to protect their heads. After an hour, they saw a white house in the distance, surrounded by some smaller buildings.

"What do you think?" Wren said.

"Too difficult to say from this distance. Looks like a farmhouse."

"We should go check it out. It might be empty. Might be just what we're looking for. A nice isolated place stuck in the middle of nowhere."

"We still need to be careful. There's nothing to say there aren't infected there."

They slowly headed towards the white buildings, partly excited, partly nervous. Could they really face more of these creatures today after what they had just been through?

When they got closer, they took a seat on a dry-stone wall under a tree and watched the house and buildings, scanning for movement, scanning for anything out of the ordinary. There was a Land Rover parked in front of the house, but there was no sign of anyone or anything. After half an hour just watching, Robyn and Wren climbed down from the wall and more cautiously than ever, began to make their way towards the property.

They ducked down as they approached the perimeter and unhitched their rucksacks, placing them behind one of the outbuildings, before scurrying round to the side and crouching even lower. They were becoming adept at field manoeuvring after just a short time on the road. They looked out from the corner across towards the farmhouse. There was still no sign of anything, and an eerie quiet befell the yard as the sunlight shone brightly on the small white stone chips.

They ran across to the house and ducked low once again, skirting along the wall, ducking underneath the windows, eventually reaching the front door. Wren crossed to the other side of it and both girls just stood there for a few seconds.

Robyn mouthed, "one, two, three," and turned the handle. They both burst through the door with their javelins raised, and that's when they saw the two shotguns pointing straight at them.

23

"Drop them now," shouted the hulking, bearded figure in front of them, as two collie dogs with wild eyes barked and snarled at their masters' side.

Robyn and Wren, out of shock more than anything, dropped the two javelins and put their hands into the air like they were on some cable tv cop show.

"Who the hell do you think you are bursting into my house?" shouted the man, whose piercing blue eyes burned holes through the two girls.

They were stuck in a stunned silence, until Robyn broke it. "I'm sorry," she said in a broken voice. She looked towards the other shotgun to see it was being held by an attractive young woman in drainpipe jeans and boots. Her black t-shirt said: "I UNDERSTAND, I JUST DON'T CARE."

The dogs continued barking wildly, and as much as the girls loved animals, they were quite unnerved by their seeming ferocity.

She looked back to the man. "I'm really sorry, we didn't know if any of those *things* would be in here. Knocking doesn't tend to be a good idea these days."

The woman laughed, "Ha, you got that right," she said lowering her gun. She reached for the barrel of the shotgun the man was still pointing at the two girls, and pushed it down. He turned to look at her sharply. "They're just girls, Dad." He lowered the shotgun further.

"Enough!" he shouted, and the two dogs immediately stopped barking and went to lie in their beds. "Well. What do you want?" he asked gruffly.

The woman raised her eyebrows. "Please forgive my dad. I'd like to say this whole end of the world thing has been an ordeal for him, but he was just like this before, too."

The back door slammed shut and an older woman and younger man walked in carrying two heavy boxes.

"What's going on here?" asked the woman, looking down at the javelins on the floor.

"We've got visitors," the younger woman replied.

The older woman put her box down on the table and pushed past the brute of a man. "And who might you two be?" She had a warm face with a red, cheery complexion.

"I'm sorry," Robyn said. "We didn't mean to barge in. We were just looking for somewhere to stay. My sister's injured and she needs to rest."

"Injured?" the woman asked, walking up to Wren. "What's wrong?"

Wren lifted her t-shirt to show the red gauze. "It was healing, but it tore this morning when…"

"When what?"

"It's a long story."

"Well don't you worry about that now. Let's get you seen to. Annie Oakley there," she said pointing towards the young woman in the black vest, "was studying to be a doctor before all this started. Let's get you into one of the bedrooms and she can take a look at you. Brendan, you get a pan of water on the stove." The younger man she had walked in with immediately headed to the sink and primed a pump before turning on the tap to fill a pan. "Thomas…" she said looking at the huge man still holding the gun by his side, "you're…no bloody use anyway at the sight of blood. You get on with whatever you were doing before our guests arrived. My name is Isabel. Come on, let's get you comfortable," she said, guiding Wren in the direction of the hallway.

"We've got rucksacks," Robyn said, almost apologetically.

"Thomas, help the young lass with her rucksacks will you?"

Robyn and Thomas left the kitchen and walked across the yard. "I am very sorry, it's just we've had a bad few days. We were watching the house for a while; we didn't think anyone was here."

There was an uncomfortable silence as the giant just walked beside her. They collected the rucksacks and headed back to the house. When they re-entered the kitchen, it was empty apart from Brendan, who was stood by the stove waiting for the pan of water.

"Is that a wood-burner?" Robyn asked.

"Yes," Brendan replied with a smile. "There's a well, too, so we've got our own water supply." The smile quickly disappeared from his face as he saw the glare from Thomas, and he turned back to the stove to watch the water.

Robyn turned to look at the big man, who simply pointed towards the hall. She guessed that was her cue to leave, and placed the rucksack down on the floor before making her way to the end bedroom. Wren was lying on the bed with her t-shirt rolled up. The younger woman was examining the wound.

"We've got some surgical alcohol and other supplies in our rucksack," Robyn said.

"Don't worry," the younger woman said, "We've got plenty."

"I'm Robyn. That's my sister, Wren."

"We've already met," the young woman said, smiling. "I'm Kayleigh, and this is my mum, Isabel."

"Nice to meet you," Robyn said.

"This wound. It's not too bad. It has stretched a little and that's caused it to start bleeding again, but it's nothing too serious. A little bit of rest and you'll be fine. I'll clean it up, put some fresh butterfly stitches and a bandage on, then you just need to take it easy," she said, looking at Wren.

"We will. As soon as we find somewhere. I appreciate you doing this after we broke into your house and everything."

"It's like you said, knocking isn't a great idea these days. So, what happened to you guys? How did you wind up here?"

Robyn began to recount their story. She was still talking long after Brendan had been in with the hot water, long after the wound had been washed and dressed, and she was still talking when Isabel and Kayleigh went back to the kitchen and began preparing dinner. By this time, Brendan and Thomas had joined them for the finale where Wren had fearlessly led all the creatures back into the doctor's surgery and made the leap of death.

"That'll probably have been Tolsta. Sounds like it, anyway," Thomas said, as he sat down at the kitchen table and the two collie dogs went to him to have a fuss made of them.

"Well, anyway, after that, we just walked and walked until we saw this place," Robyn said.

"Wow! That is some journey," Kayleigh said.

"And what were you hoping to find?" Isabel asked.

"We just want somewhere safe, and we figured there are less people in the country, so there'll be less of those things."

"Well, the two of you can stay with us for a couple of days, until Wren's wound heals, anyway," Isabel said.

"Really? Thank you. We'll be out of your hair as soon as it does, and I'll earn our keep for both of us. Anything you need doing around here, I'll do."

"Everybody works on a farm; we'll put you to good use, don't you worry."

Wren joined them at the table for dinner and they all talked until the sun went down. Robyn and Wren were given the end bedroom. They had to share a double bed, but that was not really a hardship, considering what the alternatives were.

"What do you think?" Wren whispered.

"I think they're good people. I think we're safe here. We can get a couple of good nights' sleep at least, and then when you're better, we head out and try to find a place of our own."

"Thomas scares me," Wren said.

"I think he's just quiet. It's Isabel who seems to run things."

"It's a shame. I was really hoping this place was going to be empty. It would have been perfect. Especially with the wood-burning stove and the fresh water supply. We wouldn't have wanted for anything."

"We'll find somewhere, Wren, don't worry."

*

The next morning they were woken by clattering in the kitchen. Wren looked at her watch; it was a quarter to six. "Oh man! So much for a sleep in." They quickly got dressed and headed down the hall. They were both greeted with a hail of good mornings as everyone else in the house was already up and alert. They were served plates of sausages, mushrooms, and beans with a doorstep wedge of bread and butter. By the time they had finished, it felt like their waists had expanded two sizes.

"Most important meal of the day," Isabel said, smiling. "Well, we've been talking it over, and Robyn, you're going to be helping Thomas, Brendan and Kayleigh today. Wren, you're going to be with me."

"What will we be doing?" Robyn asked.

"You'll see," Isabel said with a smile.

The two sisters looked at each other. They did not like the idea of being split up, but they were out of options. These people had welcomed them into their home, given them a bed for the night, tended Wren's wounds and fed them. Now it was time to start repaying the debt.

The dishes were cleared, the kitchen tidied, and four of them disappeared out of the door and into the waiting Land Rover. Wren stayed in the kitchen with Isabel and the dogs.

"Don't worry, they've got the hard work today; you and I have got the easy jobs," Isabel said.

"What is it you actually farm here?"

"Well, soon after the Prime Minister's speech that told us...well, you know what it told us, all our stock was bought under a compulsory purchase order. We used to farm sheep, but they all went. Y'see, an awful lot of the UK's food was imported, and when things turned bad, they brought some measures in, which, in hindsight, might not have been the smartest. But anyway, what's done is done. As well as getting paid for the sheep, they issued us with vouchers for all sorts of plants, machinery, and equipment. We exchanged ours for twenty polytunnels. What we didn't realise at the time was that the twenty polytunnels didn't actually exist. They were waiting to be manufactured. A representative actually came to visit us from the ministry of agriculture. He told us how it was going to be farms like ours which would help rebuild the country, and they were going to do everything they could to support us until things were up and running again."

"So, what happened?" Wren asked.

"Well, we got a care package to tide us over until the polytunnels were ready."

"What was the care package?"

"A cheque for a thousand pounds and a big box of assorted seeds."

"When was that?"

"About five months ago."

"And you never got the polytunnels?"

"Oh no, they arrived," Isabel said.

"When?"

"Two weeks ago."

"Oh my god! How have you survived?"

"Well, thankfully, we had a couple of sources of income. Our outgoings went down a lot. It's expensive to look after sheep…feed, vet bills, and so on. We managed. We went back to a lot of the old ways. How Thomas's dad and grandad survived. This place has been in the family for generations."

"But things will be okay now though? I mean you can start growing again?"

Isabel laughed. "Eventually."

"What do you mean? I thought the Polytunnels had arrived."

"The components have, Wren. They don't come ready assembled. That's where your sister's going today. She's going to help with putting the first one up."

"So how long will that take?"

"I don't ask Thomas things like that. He's not a man of many words, and often when I ask a question, I wish I hadn't bothered. It will be done when it's done."

"And what are we going to do?"

"Well, I don't see the supermarket opening anytime soon, so you and I are going to do a different type of food shopping," Isabel said, smiling.

"I don't understand."

"You will."

Isabel placed a large shopping bag over her shoulder, and a backpack over the other one, carefully placing one of the shotguns inside. They walked out into the yard, and even though it was early, the blueness of the sky told them it was going to be another beautiful day. Wren followed Isabel across to one of the outbuildings. She disappeared for a short time only to re-emerge with two fishing rods.

"We're going fishing?"

"Among other things."

＊

The four of them broke for lunch at just past twelve o'clock. They were dripping in sweat as the sun beat down. They had been digging and preparing the ground to lay the foundation for the first polytunnel. Thomas was the only one who truly knew what he was doing and he had to give constant instructions to the others, but he was content that they were good workers and not taking that much more time that a team of builders would take.

They passed a large bottle of water between them and ate thick slices of bread covered generously with homemade damson jam. "You work well for someone from the city," Thomas said.

"I had a part-time job before. My dad always said there's no point doing something unless you give it your all, no matter what it is," Robyn said.

The big man nodded appreciatively. "Sounds like a smart man. Lots of work to do here...lots." He said looking at the masses of frames and thick Perspex sheets that were piled in one corner of the field. "Going to take some time." Robyn didn't know what to say; she just nodded and handed the bottle of water back to him. He took another long drink before climbing back to his feet. "Well, the day's wasting," he said, getting back to work.

"I think you just got Dad's nod of approval," Kayleigh said, smiling.

＊

It was late afternoon when Isabel, Wren, and the dogs began their journey back from the river. They had spent the day sat on the river banks getting to know each other and trying to catch dinner. Having managed to bag three decent-sized salmon, their mission was accomplished. Now as they walked back through the woods, Isabel came to a stop and pulled out a plastic bag from her backpack. She stood in front of a tree whose branches looked like they were dying, and cut off big clusters of strange-looking mushrooms.

"Aren't they poisonous?" Wren asked, watching her.

"There are lots of poisonous mushrooms and toadstools; you really need to know what you're doing, but these, my dear, are most definitely not poisonous. In fact, when I fry these for us, I can guarantee you'll be looking out for them from now on."

Wren examined them a little more closely. "I've never seen anything like that in our local supermarket."

Isabel let out a chuckle. "I dare say. The sheer wealth of what you can eat from the wilds that you don't see in the supermarket would shock you." She finished removing the mushrooms and held the healthy-looking collection up in front of her. "I mean, look at this place for example," she said, gesturing around the woods. You've got nettles for nettle soup; Hawthorns, you can eat the leaves and the berries; Ramsons…you put those in stews, casseroles, and soups for flavouring, and that's just what I can see standing here. There is a world of food that people don't eat anymore. Don't worry, we've got a few tins in the cupboards at home, and we've got some spuds growing out back and a few other bits and pieces, but if we save as much of that stuff as we can for a rainy day and live off the woods and the river until the polytunnels start producing, we're going to be fine."

"It sounds like you've got it all planned. I hope we can find a place near here so Bobbi and I can come visit."

Isabel looked at her long and hard before breaking out into a wide smile.

"Come on, let's get back. The workforce will want their dinner on the table for when they get home."

"Thank you for today, Isabel. I've enjoyed it," Wren said.

"How are you feeling?"

"I feel good. The wound feels fine."

"Another couple of days and you should be a lot better."

Wren smiled, not wanting to think about going back out on the road for the time being.

*

They all ate well that night, the conversation flowed, and it was with reluctance that they left the dinner table. Robyn and Wren insisted on clearing the dishes and washed them in clean, albeit cold, water. They made tea which they drank with powdered milk, and Wren brought out the last packet of Oreos from her rucksack for everybody to share round. Before everyone made their way to bed, Isabel embraced the two sisters and told Wren they would try a different spot and catch even more salmon tomorrow.

In bed, Wren and Robyn recounted the events of the day to each other before passing out with tired but contented smiles.

A knock at the door woke them up the following morning. Light was already pouring in through the curtains, and Isabel came into the room carrying mugs of tea for them both. The two sisters quickly sat up in bed, and Isabel set the tea down on the bedside table and turned to the girls with a serious look on her face.

"When you've got washed and dressed, will you come and join Thomas and me in the kitchen?" she said before heading back out of the room.

Robyn and Wren looked at each other with concern. Were they being sent back out on the road already? They did as they were asked, and walked into the kitchen with trepidation. Thomas and Isabel were sat at the table waiting for them.

"We're going on a little ride," Thomas said, standing up and taking the car keys from the peg on the wall.

Wren looked at her watch; it was just past six o'clock and there was no sign of Kayleigh or Brendan. "Is something wrong?" she asked, as she and Robyn followed Thomas out to the Land Rover.

"You two get in the back, Her Majesty always rides in the front," he said, with something approaching a smile on his face. Some people did not suit smiles, and it was almost as if Thomas was trying his on for the first time.

Isabel climbed into the front seat and put on her seatbelt. "Where are we going?" Robyn asked.

"You'll see," Isabel replied without turning around.

Wren looked at her sister. *What was going on?* Both of them began to feel nervous. The Land Rover started and pulled out of the yard and onto the road. It travelled for about ninety seconds before turning left, and up a small drive. The drive led to a wide gate, and beyond the gate stood a white cottage, beyond the cottage was a small loch. Even at this time of morning with a new hot day looming, the midges were out in force and Wren and Robyn batted them away as they got out of the car.

Thomas brought out another key from his pocket and opened the front door. They all walked in; there was a small table in the entrance with a selection of leaflets about what to do and where to visit in the surrounding area. Next to them, there was a red, leather-bound book with *Visitors* on the front in gold lettering. Isabel led them farther down the hall and into the living room, which had hardwood floors and a large, wood-burning stove. She opened the patio doors and they stepped out onto a small decked area. In front of them was a lawn that led down to the loch. There was a path at either side of the house, and beyond that lay woodland.

"What is this place?" Wren asked.

"You know I told you we had other forms of income? Well, we own a couple of holiday cottages in the area. This is one of them, only, I doubt we're going to get many bookings any time soon."

"I guess not," Wren replied, looking out over the shimmering loch.

"Thomas and I were talking, and we think it would be a good idea if you two moved in here. You'll help us get the polytunnels up, you'll help us with stuff around the farm, and in return, you can live here and you can get a share of the produce. Enough to make sure you're fed properly. You can help when we cut wood, and you can have some for your stove. And if you need our help, we're both just a stone's throw away.

The two girls were still looking out over the beautiful loch and beyond to the woods. When they turned back around, they both had tears running down their faces. Wren threw her arms around Isabel and Robyn threw hers around Thomas, which was a little like throwing them around a very wide oak tree. He stood there for a moment, frozen, not quite knowing how to respond to this girl who had him stuck in an emotional bear hug. He put his right arm around her, then his left, and gently returned the hug with a little pat to her back.

"You've no idea what this means to us," Wren said.

Isabel kissed the top of her head. "It usually takes me a while to warm up to people, but I liked both of you from the start. If the last few days have taught us anything, it's that we never know when our time is up. It would be stupid to waste it now, wouldn't it?"

EPILOGUE

It had been a good day. They had got the frame for the first of the polytunnels standing, and it would not be long before the rest of it was up and they could start planting. Although never having had one before, Thomas knew lots of farmers and smallholders who had, and he knew the crops that grew the fastest. Spinach, kale, rocket, courgettes, lettuce…there were many. The family was going to be self-sufficient in no time, and then, they would get more tunnels up and begin to trade. He was sure there would be other outlying farms who had escaped the horrors of the towns and cities.

As he pulled the Land Rover into the farmyard, his brow furrowed.

"Who the hell's that?" Kayleigh said as the four of them looked towards the 7.5-tonne truck parked outside the house. Thomas pulled on the handbrake and they all climbed out.

"Stay here," he said opening the back and pulling out the shotgun. He walked towards the door and Brendan joined him, but he put a hand on his shoulder. "Keep an eye on the girls." Thomas placed his fingers on the handle

204

and pushed the door open, ready to raise the shotgun at the first sign of trouble.

"Will you put that thing away?" Isabel said as all the heads at the table spun towards the doorway. Wren was sat at the far end and two strangers, one a middle-aged man, one a younger man, were sat with their backs to the door. They looked a little startled as they turned and saw a giant with a shotgun standing in the doorway, boring holes through them with his eyes.

"I didn't expect visitors," Thomas said, walking into the kitchen and putting the shotgun on one of the countertops.

"This is...I'm sorry, I've forgotten your name already," Isabel said.

The man stood up and walked over to Thomas. "McKeith, Gordon McKeith. I'm pleased to meet you, Thomas. Your wife has been telling me all about you and what you're doing here."

Thomas raised an eyebrow and looked at Isabel. He extended his hand, and the two men shook. "I don't recognise you from these parts."

"Well, no, me and the lad here are from up in Loch Uig. We managed to escape a large part of what hit everybody else by the sound of it," he said returning to his seat.

"Loch Uig? I'd heard that place had been taken over by an armed gang."

McKeith and the younger man burst out laughing. "And that's without fake news and the internet. I've heard all sorts since I took to the road. No, Loch Uig is as it always was. Like I say, it faired a lot better than most."

"And what are you doing down here?" Thomas asked.

"Well, as I was explaining to Isabel, I'm wanting to see who's around, see who's in a position to trade. We've got requirements up there, like anybody. By the sounds of it, in a few months, you'll be flourishing again. Maybe we could trade what we have for some of what you have.

"And what do you have, exactly?" Thomas asked as Brendan, Kayleigh and Robyn walked through the door.

"We're still taking stock, but I was happy to make a trade with your wife already," he said, smiling towards Isabel.

"Is that right?"

"We've got a cheesemaker up there, and we still have a few dairy cows. I wanted to show goodwill and prove I was serious, so I traded a wheel of our local cheese for a bucket of spuds. Trust me, it's a good cheese. Maybe when I come back, we can trade a lot more."

Thomas turned to look at the large circle of cheese on the counter and he almost started salivating before turning back to McKeith. "Maybe," he replied.

There was a long silence, But McKeith broke it. "Well, thank you for your hospitality, and thank you for letting me know about Tolsta. I'll be sure to avoid it." They all shook hands and he left carrying the bucket of potatoes. He put them in the back of the truck before climbing into the driver's side.

The engine started and the stone chips crackled as the truck pulled away. McKeith looked in the mirror as the family was assembled in the doorway. He lowered the window and leaned out, giving them a friendly wave before putting it back up. He smiled to himself and turned the wheel right. Their journey was underway once more. They had only been gone from Loch Uig one day, but already they had covered so much ground. The rural communities had fared much better than the towns and cities and now his plans were coming to fruition.

"I still don't understand why we traded all that cheese for just a few spuds," the younger man said.

"I wouldn't expect you to," McKeith replied.

"Well?"

"I don't answer to you."

"No, but when you show up with less than you set out with, The Boss is going to be happy as Larry to see you."

McKeith turned to look at his passenger. In one violent movement, he grabbed hold of the back of the younger man's head and smashed it against the dashboard. There was a loud crack, the young man screamed and as he brought his head back up, blood poured from his nose.

"What somebody like you will never understand is the most valuable currency is information. What we gave them in a bit of cheese we're going to earn a thousand times over when we come back down here and take their harvest...and those women. Watch and learn boy, watch and learn."

THE END.

CHRISTOPHER ARTINIAN

A NOTE FROM THE AUTHOR

I really hope you enjoyed this book and would be very grateful if you took a minute to leave a review on Amazon and Goodreads.

If you would like to stay informed about what I'm doing, including current writing projects, and all the latest news and release information; these are the places to go:

Join the fan club on Facebook
https://www.facebook.com/groups/127693634504226

Like the Christopher Artinian author page
https://www.facebook.com/safehaventrilogy/

Buy exclusive and signed books and merchandise, subscribe to the newsletter and follow the blog:
https://www.christopherartinian.com/

Follow me on Twitter
https://twitter.com/Christo71635959

Follow me on Amazon
https://amzn.to/2I1llU6

Follow me on Goodreads
https://bit.ly/2P7iDzX

Other books by Christopher Artinian:

Safe Haven: Rise of the RAMs
Safe Haven: Realm of the Raiders
Safe Haven: Reap of the Righteous
Safe Haven: Ice
Before Safe Haven: Lucy
Before Safe Haven: Alex
Before Safe Haven: Mike

Anthologies featuring short stories by Christopher Artinian

Undead Worlds: A Reanimated Writers Anthology
Featuring: Before Safe Haven: Losing the Battle by Christopher Artinian
Tales from Zombie Road: The Long-Haul Anthology
Featuring: Condemned by Christopher Artinian

Treasured Chests: A Zombie Anthology for Breast Cancer Care

Featuring: Last Light by Christopher Artinian

Trick or Treat Thrillers (Best Paranormal 2018)
Featuring: The Akkadian Vessel.

CHRISTOPHER ARTINIAN

Christopher Artinian was born and raised in Leeds, West Yorkshire. Wanting to escape life in a big city and concentrate more on working to live than living to work, he and his family moved to the Outer Hebrides in the north-west of Scotland in 2004, where he now works as a full-time author.

Chris is a huge music fan, a cinephile, an avid reader and a supporter of Yorkshire county cricket club. When he's not sat in front of his laptop living out his next post-apocalyptic/dystopian/horror adventure, he will be passionately immersed in one of his other interests.

Printed in Great Britain
by Amazon

86839133R00130